Dear God,

How are you? I am not doing fine. Not at all. Yesterday Solomon got sick with something and fell, and he is really bad. He might not live. The worst part is how sad Erin is. She is trying to be brave, but I know she has ridden Solomon all her life, and she loves him a lot. Please don't let him die. Also, I did go to church today. I liked the singing, but I felt sort of strange. I didn't know anyone, and I couldn't follow the teacher too well. Plus, I feel as if I'm butting in on Erin's church friends. None of them is her Secret Sister, though.

Tess stopped writing for a minute and reached into her pants pocket, pulling out the pack of gum. She carefully unwrapped a piece and licked the powder off the surface before popping the gum into her mouth. She smiled at the thought of Erin chewing her gum, too.

Might as well talk about the really scary part. It wasn't as if God didn't already know.

But worst of all, something horrible is happening to Mom. She fainted this afternoon, and she's been really crabby. Her face is all white. Please, God, don't let anything bad happen to my mom. Please make her well. I know you can. Thank you.

Love, Tess

Secret Sisters: (se'-krit sis'-terz) n. Two friends who choose each other to be everything a real sister should be: loyal and loving. They share with and help each other no matter what!

Secret ✦ Sisters

Star Light

Sandra Byrd

WATERBROOK
PRESS
COLORADO SPRINGS

STAR LIGHT

PUBLISHED BY WATERBROOK PRESS

5446 North Academy Boulevard, Suite 200

Colorado Springs, Colorado 80918

A division of Random House, Inc.

ISBN 1-57856-017-9

Published in association with the literary agency of Janet
Kobobel Grant, Books & Such, 3093 Maiden Lane, Altadena,
CA 91001.

2000

3 5 7 9 10 8 6 4

To Joye Davis

When it's dark enough, you can see the stars.
—Ralph Waldo Emerson

one

Down for the Count

Saturday, November 16

"Hey, lizard lips." Tess Thomas tapped the glass cage of Hercules, her eight-year-old-brother Tyler's horned toad.

Hercules flicked his tongue at her in disdain.

"I thought he wasn't supposed to be in the kitchen anymore," she said to Tyler as he walked into the room.

"He's not. I was just moving him," Tyler said, lugging the heavy cage from the room. "Where are you going?"

"To Erin's grandma and grandpa's to ride horses, if Dad hurries up. I'm supposed to be there in fifteen minutes. We're already late." Tess stopped pacing the pale yellow floor long enough to glance out the patio door, scanning the yard to see if her father had finished with the pool. Although the autumn weather was sunny and mild in Scottsdale, Arizona, it wasn't warm enough to swim anymore. Mr. Thomas was storing all the pool stuff for the winter. She sighed in relief as he closed and locked the shed door and headed toward the house.

"Ta ta, cheerio, and all that. I'm sure you'll have fun, but not as much fun as I will. Big Al and I are going to the Chocolate Chipper to play mini-golf."

"Big Al! I don't know what you see in that kid. He lives to be gross."

Tess and Big Al had a hate-hate relationship. He hated to see her, and she hated to see him. Tyler, however, liked Al a lot.

Tess studied her brother with affection. One unruly cowlick sprang from his otherwise smooth brown hair, and his lightly freckled face was almost always happy.

"Steady on, old girl. He has a good side only I know."

"Back to the English accent, eh?" Tess teased. Tyler loved British mysteries on television and often spoke like his favorite sleuths.

Tyler shrugged her off and left the kitchen as Mr. Thomas squeaked open the sliding glass door and asked, "Ready to go?"

"Yep. Let's head out. I don't want to be too late. They might go riding without me." She didn't really believe Erin would leave without her, but Tess was eager to get moving. She slipped her arms into an old, patched jeans jacket and pulled her long brown hair out from under the collar. It spilled in coarse waves over her shoulders, cascading several inches down her back.

After Mr. Thomas plucked his keys from the hook near the back door, he opened the automatic garage door. A few minutes later the Jeep was on the way to

Gilbert, the small town in which Erin's grandparents lived.

"Um, Dad?" Tess started hesitantly. She stared out the window, pretending to be interested in the Indian reservation as they passed by it. The Pima tribe had lived here for maybe a thousand years. Now it was squeezed onto a reservation the size of a former village. The emptiness of the Indians' land contrasted with the closely built homes of the city, just across the road.

"Yes?"

"Did I tell you Erin asked me to go to church with her tomorrow morning?"

Her father waited a minute before answering. "Hmm. What did you say?"

"I told her I would need to talk with you and Mom about it." Still looking out the window, Tess concentrated her eyes on the fresh-vegetable stands offering squash, pumpkins, and shriveled dates for sale. If she looked at her dad, he might see how tense she was.

"I don't know, Tess. This church thing seems to be getting out of hand. I mean, it's fine to go to a party, but you know Sunday mornings are family time for us."

She finally turned toward him to speak. "I know, but I'd really like to go. I met a lot of kids at the Harvest Party last month, and I'd like to see some of them again. I would be home before lunch." Tess nervously picked at a hangnail as she waited in the uncomfortable silence. If her dad felt this bad about her going to church, what would he say when she finally worked up enough nerve to tell him she had decided to become a Christian?

"I don't know. I want to talk with her parents first. I don't want you mixed up with a cult or anything."

"Dad, it's perfectly okay. It's a normal church. Don't you trust me?" Squinting through the early afternoon sun, she smiled at her father. Jim Thomas was a tall, athletically built man with a dimpled chin that lent a youthful look to his handsome face, despite his thinning hair.

"Yes, kiddo, I trust you. But I'll still talk with her parents."

Fifteen minutes later, after some light chitchat about school, her dad asked, "Do I turn somewhere around here?"

"It's a few blocks away. I've only been here a couple of times. I hope I can remember." It was bad enough to leave late, but now if she got them lost, they would be really late, maybe holding everyone else up.

Erin, her best friend and Secret Sister, invited Tess to ride horses at Erin's grandparents' ranch whenever she could. Tess hadn't ridden often, but she was getting better at it. Usually she rode Solomon, the older, chocolate-brown horse with creamy white socks. Tess and Erin had been best pals for only a couple of months, but already they knew they were lifetime friends. That's why they had decided to be Secret Sisters. Since they both had only brothers, they had chosen one another as sisters, and they did everything for each other that a sister would do. But in secret! And since last month, when Tess had decided to give Jesus control of her life, they were "real" sisters now: spiritual sisters. Tess was eager to spend the day with her sis.

"I think this is it." Tess pointed toward a long, winding dirt road that led into the ranch. Cholla cactus stood guard, one on each side of the dusty driveway. Their fat, spiny arms ushered Tess and her dad down the road.

"This is a nice place! One of the few that hasn't been developed into houses, I see," her father commented.

"I know. Erin said lots of people have asked her grandparents to sell, but they just can't do it. They've been here a long time, and it wouldn't seem right. I'm glad, too." Tess glanced out the window, wondering if Tom would be around today. Tom was Erin's older brother, and Tess thought he was, well, pretty special. She didn't exactly have a crush on him, but he was cute and nice, and all the things she would look for if she did have a crush on someone. He played basketball for the middle school, so he might be at practice today. Oh, well. There would be other times.

"I wonder whose truck that is?" Tess leaned forward to see better. "I thought Erin said no one besides her family was going to be here. Maybe her uncle came or something."

A long, oversized, red pickup was parked just outside the corral and barn entrance. As they drove closer, Tess could read the words, "Dave Wenzel, D.V.M."

"What does D.V.M. mean?" she asked.

"Doctor of Veterinary Medicine," Jim Thomas answered, pulling the Jeep alongside the truck.

As he did, Tess could see a crowd gathered inside the corral. "I wonder what's going on?" She unbuckled her seat belt.

"I don't know," her dad answered. "But I'll come with you."

As she climbed from the car, Tess strained to see beyond the crowd of people gathered in the center of the corral. What was it? She saw a hoof, then the horse lying on his side.

"Oh no!" she gasped. "Solomon is down on the ground. And look!" In an awful moment she saw what everyone was really concerned about. There, in the dust, with her legs twisted and eyes closed, lay Erin.

two

Founder

Saturday, November 16

"It's okay, hon." Tess's dad rested his arm reassuringly on her shoulder, but she paid little attention.

"Erin!" she called, dropping her backpack before running toward the corral.

Erin must have heard her, because she turned her head and opened her eyes, looking dazed but searching for Tess. "Tess? Is that you?" Erin peered beyond the crowd encircling her.

"Yes." Tess arrived at her side and kneeled beside her. "What happened?"

"I'm—I'm not sure," Erin said, trying to prop herself up on her elbows. "Mom?" She looked toward her mother.

"First of all, are you okay? Can you see straight?" Mrs. Janssen bent down beside Erin, helped her sit up, and checked her head for any lumps or bruises.

"Yes, I'm okay. I can see all right. I do feel a little shaky."

After reassuring herself that her daughter was fine, Mrs. Janssen explained what had happened. As she did, Tess's dad ducked under the wood fence to meet them in the corral. "Well, we asked Dr. Wenzel to come over today because Solomon has been limping a bit, and we thought he might have twisted his leg. At first he seemed okay, and Erin offered to take him for a gentle walk around the corral so Dr. Wenzel could evaluate his gait. All of a sudden Solomon wobbled and then collapsed. Oh, Erin!" Her mother clasped her close. "I'm so glad you seem to be all right! What was I thinking, allowing you to ride him?" A small gasp caught in Mrs. Janssen's throat, and Tess could see she was about to cry.

"Now, Nancy." Erin's dad patted his wife's shoulder. "We had no idea Solomon was so weak. Look, he's trying to get up now."

Just as Erin was standing up on her shaky legs, Solomon was trying to stand as well. After his hooves trampled the dust a bit, he finally did stand, but it was clear he was in pain. Dr. Wenzel coached Solomon back into the barn, and everyone watched him limp along.

"Are you okay?" Erin's dad asked her.

"Yeah, Dad, I am." She brushed the dust from her clothes. "But what about Solomon?"

"I'm not sure. Why don't you and Tess go into the house with Mom and Grandma for a minute, and I'll wait out here with Grandpa until Dr. Wenzel finishes his examination. Would you like to wait out here, too?" He motioned to Tess's dad.

"Yes, Jim Thomas here. Nice to meet you." He held out his hand.

"Ned Janssen. Likewise." Erin's father shook his hand in return, and they ambled toward the barn.

"Can I help you? Do you want to lean on me?" Tess asked her friend, who was limping slightly.

"No, I think I'll be okay. Sorry about this." Erin grimaced at Tess.

"Don't worry about it! I'm just glad you're okay." After patting her friend on the shoulder, Tess glanced at the sky. The sun was shining merrily, and little puffs of clouds tooted across a pale blue sky like the little train that thought it could. But in reality, things were not sunny but very bad. Solomon must be really sick.

Erin's grandma and grandpa lived in a rustic western ranch home. Thick planked beams supported the stuccoed ceiling, and the polished wood floor was dotted with Native American rugs. The wide kitchen table was fashioned of dark oak, and a hand-sculpted pottery vase, painted by local craftswomen, graced its center. After the family and Tess pulled their chairs up to the table, Grandma poured frothy root beer into cowboy-boot-shaped glasses. When the foam died down, Tess took a long drink, savoring the sweet, piney liquid as it covered her tongue.

Erin's mom brushed her daughter's hair away from her eyes and said, "Honey, I'm sorry, but I don't think we should ride today. This has everyone a little shook up. Maybe Tess could come next week."

"Yeah, Mom, I know. I feel a little dizzy anyway. Sorry, Sis." Erin smiled sadly at Tess.

"No problem," Tess said, glad that her friend hadn't been crushed by the falling horse.

Only the occasional slurping of soda broke the silence. After a few minutes the men came back into the house. Through the window Tess could see the vet leaving.

"Well?" Erin asked. "Is he okay? I mean, the vet was able to fix him and everything, right?"

"I'm afraid it's not that simple," her dad answered. "Dr. Wenzel said Solomon has founder, which is a dangerous disease. Horses are particularly susceptible after eating a lot of fall or spring foliage. See how tall the grasses are out there?" They all glanced out the window at the long, slender reeds waving in the wind. "The weather has been so rainy this fall that the grasses are lush and long. Maybe Solomon will heal, maybe he won't. Only a little time will tell."

"Oh, but he won't die, will he?" Erin asked.

Tess saw a look of pain shadow Erin's grandpa's face. "We don't know. We just don't know. But we will in a week or so. Until then, we can pray."

A lump caught in Tess's throat as she saw a tear tremble on Erin's lashes before trickling down her cheek. Tess reached across the table and patted Erin's hand.

"It'll be okay. I'll pray, too," Tess said.

"Thank you," Erin responded, but she didn't seem encouraged.

"Well, Tess, we'd better get back home," said her dad, breaking the silence. "It looks as though Erin might need a bit of rest today."

"Okay. Just a minute." Tess ran out to the corral where she had dropped her backpack. She turned around, ready to race back to the house, but changed her mind. Quietly she slipped into the barn and looked at Solomon, who lay in his stall with his eyes closed.

"Bye, boy," she whispered, tears popping out unexpectedly. "Get well soon. And thanks for being so easy on me." She slipped back out and hauled her backpack into the house.

❊

"Here," she said to Erin, "I brought you the book you wanted to borrow. Maybe this will take your mind off Solomon for a little while." Tess smiled at Erin, and she smiled back, but just a little.

"Thanks. Are you still coming to church with me tomorrow?" Erin looked up hopefully.

Tess glanced over to her dad, who nodded slightly. "Yes, I am. What time will you pick me up?"

"Nine forty-five. I'm so glad you can come. Don't forget; we're both wearing blue."

"I won't. See you tomorrow."

During the ride home, Tess spoke first. "Thanks for letting me go tomorrow, Dad."

"You're welcome. I didn't have a chance to talk with

her parents about the church, what with everything else going on, but I couldn't say no after today's disappointments. I'll talk with them about it later this week. Erin's dad seems like a decent kind of guy. I didn't know he was the chef at Red Rocks Resort. Fancy place."

They settled into the drive, making plans for a difficult hike this week to prepare them for the Grand Canyon Rim-to-Rim hike next May. Tess was glad her dad didn't bring up the subject of church again because, to tell the truth, she was a little nervous about going. What if she felt stupid? What if no one talked with her? What if the teacher asked her a lot of questions and she didn't know any of the answers? She could only hope it would be okay.

three

Something Borrowed, Something Blue

Sunday, November 17

"Can I please borrow your blue sweater?" Tess pleaded with her mom.

Usually a lighthearted woman, today Molly Thomas seemed downright crabby. "I don't know, Tess. Every time I let you borrow some of my clothes, they end up either stained or rolled up in a ball under your bed. I have to go on a massive hunt to find them, and when I finally do, they're dirty, and I can't wear them anyway." She pulled her hair into a loose ponytail and studied the result in her bedroom mirror.

"I promise that won't happen. Nothing will spill on it. I promise. I'll come right home from church and change and hang it up in your closet. I want to look nice, and none of my stuff looks right," Tess pleaded.

"Oh, all right," her mom answered wearily. She slipped her feet into her wool slippers and padded toward the kitchen.

Grabbing the sweater, Tess dashed back to her own room to finish dressing. A few minutes later she heard gravel crunching in front of the house and looked out her window. Erin was here! A sick feeling filled Tess's stomach like a water balloon slogging around inside her. Did she really want to go? She was eager to learn more about Jesus but afraid she would feel foolish around people who had gone to church for a long time. Maybe they could tell by looking at her that she hadn't.

"Hey, where are you going?" Tyler shouted from the family room, his voice rising above the blaring cartoons.

"Church," Tess answered.

"What?"

"Church!" Tess poked her head into the family room on her way to the door.

"Steady on, old girl. No need to holler. That's what I thought you said. I just couldn't believe it." He bit into his toast, and a long thread of rhubarb jam smeared across his chin. He licked it and turned back to the TV. Tess rolled her eyes, then headed out the door.

"Hi, how are you feeling this morning?" she asked Erin as Erin's dad pulled the car out of the driveway. Living Waters Community Church was only a few minutes from Tess's house.

"Good, except for this." Erin pointed at a black-and-blue spot next to her right eye.

"Ouch! Does it hurt?"

"A little. Did you bring a Bible?"

"No, was I supposed to?" Tess asked nervously. Great. She had already blown it. She would be the only one there without a Bible. "I don't think we have one. Well, maybe. I think my grandfather's old Bible is under the TV cabinet. But I'm not sure."

"It's okay. You can share mine." Erin patted a blue-jeans case.

"What's that, your Bible?" Tess fingered the worn cover with a pocket on the outside. Pens and lip gloss stuffed the pocket.

"Yep. My mom made it out of an old pair of Levi's. Cool, huh?" Erin uncapped a lip gloss and smoothed it over her lips. "Want some?"

"Sure," Tess said.

"Gross!" Josh, Erin's eight-year-old brother, piped in. "That's disgusting, like sharing a toothbrush."

"No it's not, goofus," Erin said.

"Where's Tom?" Tess tried to act casual as she asked, but her voice cracked a little.

"He got a ride with his friends." Erin must have seen a look of disappointment cross Tess's face because she continued, "But he'll come home with us. Don't worry."

Tess shot her a mad look, which meant, *Don't laugh or say anything in front of your parents!*

Erin elbowed her mischievously, and Tess smiled as they pulled into the church parking lot.

Tess had been to the church once before, last month when Erin had invited her to the Harvest Party. After a night of fun games, singing, and food, Tess had decided church wasn't so bad after all. The only bad part about that night was losing her mom's earrings, but it had all worked out okay in the end. Coming for something serious, though, on Sunday, seemed a lot riskier than a party. Tess gulped anxiously as she said a silent prayer.

"Do we sit in the church with all the adults?" she asked.

"No," Erin said. "At our church we don't actually go into the main service until high school. We have our own time of worship and a lesson in the Sunday school class."

Tess breathed a bit easier. It would be better with fewer people.

A long gray corridor led to the sixth-grade Sunday school class. World maps lined the hallways, with little gold foil stars marking spots on each map.

"What are those stars?" Tess asked.

"They show where my church supports missionaries. You know, like the ones who visited last month and told the twenty-one ponies story," Erin answered.

"That's a lot of places!"

The classroom was cheery and full. Almost as many sixth graders were here as were in her class at Coronado Elementary School. Long and wide, the room held at least fifty chairs set up in half circles. Up front the teacher's podium stood silent guard over an overhead projector and a chalkboard. A big CD player with four speakers sat to one side.

How could so many sixth graders go to one church? Tess thought of the only time she had gone to church with her grandparents in Minnesota. About fifty people attended that church. With all the people here, Tess was feeling smaller and smaller, like Alice in Wonderland.

"Erin, what happened to your face?" A loud girl ran up to Erin, bowling into Tess as she did. Suddenly, a crowd gathered around Erin as she told the group about Solomon.

"Will he live?" one guy asked.

"We're not sure. I hope so," Erin answered, sniffing a bit.

"We'll pray about it," someone else promised. Just then everyone seemed to look at Tess, who had been standing quietly behind Erin.

"Oh, this is Tess," Erin said. "She's visiting today."

Everyone said hello to Tess, but she still felt dumb. She hoped Erin wouldn't tell everyone that she was a new Christian. Of course, she didn't need to worry. Erin said nothing.

During the opening lesson, Tess looked around the room, searching for anyone she had met at the party last month. She thought she recognized a few faces, but she wasn't sure, and they were on the other side of the room. Doodling on the back of a piece of paper from Erin's notebook, Tess felt left out. The teacher had some good things to say, and Tess wrote down a couple of them to think about later, but she didn't feel connected. So many words she didn't understand! Sometimes the discussion was a little boring. After the lesson, they sang, and even though she didn't know the songs, she caught on quickly.

Tess liked that part. The music was great, not slow oldies stuff. And everyone sounded so natural when they prayed, like actual talking.

She reached into her pocket and felt something hard. She had forgotten. Pulling out a pack of gum, she slipped it to Erin.

"What's this?" Erin whispered.

"Sister gum," Tess whispered back. "I thought of it last night. Whenever you chew a piece, think of me. I got some for myself, too. See?" She held up an identical pack of gum. "Whenever I chew it, I'll think of you. And I'll pray for you," she added. "And for Solomon."

"Great idea. I'm so glad you came," Erin said.

Soon the class was over, and Tess and Erin went over to the snack table. Tess helped herself to a glass of the ruby-red punch. The noisy girl came barreling over again, eager to get next to Erin. It bugged Tess.

"Hey, Erin!" The girl pushed closer, bumping Tess as she did. She jarred Tess's hand. In an awful instant, Tess saw what was about to happen but couldn't stop it. The punch made perfect contact with its target: her mother's blue sweater.

"Oh, sorry. Here, have a napkin." The girl practically threw one at Tess and turned back to Erin.

Erin talked for a minute, then turned to Tess. "Are you okay?" she asked.

"Yes," Tess said, although she really wasn't. Her mom was going to kill her.

"We'd better go. My family will be waiting."

They made their way out past what seemed like a thousand strangers waiting in the church's foyer.

"I hope you can come next week, too. Did you have a good time?" Erin asked hopefully.

What could Tess say? She thought it was okay but not really fun. Was it supposed to be fun? She didn't know and didn't want to hurt Erin's feelings. And what about the sweater!

"It was okay," Tess answered honestly. But inside she was upset. She felt like an outsider, and she wasn't sure she would ever fit in. Did this mean she couldn't be a Christian after all?

four

Dear...Who?

Sunday Afternoon, November 17

"I'm home!" Tess called out as she heaved the front door shut.

"Please don't slam the door!" her mother called out. "It shakes the pictures on the wall."

Tess plodded into the kitchen. "What are you doing?"

"Making sandwiches." Her mother spread tuna salad over slices of honey oat bread. She made the best tuna salad, chopping little pieces of grapes in with the tuna and mayonnaise. "Why don't you go change?" Mrs. Thomas asked.

"Oh yeah," Tess said. "Well, there was a little accident." *Here goes*, she thought.

"What kind of accident?" Her mom stopped spreading.

"A girl spilled juice on your sweater. I'm sorry, Mom. It wasn't my fault." Tess looked at her mother's face, which had gone pale. Man, Tess hadn't thought it would be that big a deal. "Mom?" she asked as her mother swayed a bit and set down the knife.

"I feel faint," her mom said, heading toward the nearest chair. "I'm going to sit here for a minute. Can you finish up the sandwiches, please? And get the chips out of the cupboard."

"Okay. Are you all right?" Tess was getting nervous. Her mom was never tired this time of day. Her face looked chalk-dust white.

"I'll be okay in a minute." Just as her mom said the last word, her head dropped with a thump on the table.

"Mom! Mom!" Tess ran over to her. Tess's suddenly cold hands smoothed her mother's hair back from her face, but her mother didn't respond.

"Help! Dad, Tyler, anyone!" Tess yelled toward the family room. "Quick, somebody! Something bad has happened to Mom!"

Her father and Ty came running into the room. "Molly?" Mr. Thomas called, reaching the table. He grabbed the phone.

"She passed out on the table, and she won't wake up," Tess told him.

Just then her mother mumbled something and slowly lifted her head. Mr. Thomas set down the phone and bent down beside her chair.

"I don't know what happened," she finally said. "I was listening to Tess, and suddenly her voice got softer and very far away, and I felt lightheaded. So I sat down, and the next thing I knew, you all were standing around me."

"Let's call the doctor," Tyler said. He was nervous, switching his weight back and forth between his feet.

"That's not a bad idea," their dad said.

"No, no," Mrs. Thomas insisted. "It's Sunday, and no one is in. I'd have to go to the emergency room, and I don't want to do that. We just went last month." She smiled tiredly at Tess.

Last month Tess had set the kitchen on fire while trying to fry chicken. She had ended up frying the wallpaper and her hand instead.

"I'm just tired. Why don't I go lie down, and you guys can finish up. I'll see the doctor tomorrow if I'm not feeling better. It's the start of flu season. Maybe I've caught a bug." She shuffled off to her room. Tess, Tyler, and their father all looked at each other, helpless.

"Well, we have to eat," their father said. "Tess, you finish the sandwiches. Ty, you get out the juice, and I'll find some paper plates."

They all choked down their food but didn't say much.

"How was church?" Tyler asked, trying to make conversation but forgetting his British accent what with everything else going on.

"It was okay," Tess said. "About fifty kids in the sixth grade were there."

"Wow, that's amazing." Tyler's appetite apparently was returning. He stuffed the last bit of his sandwich into his mouth.

"Did you meet anyone new?" her dad asked. But he wasn't looking at Tess. He was peering down the hall where Tess's mom had just gone to bed.

"No, not really."

After a few, uncomfortable minutes, her dad said, "I guess I'll check on Mom."

"I think I'll do some homework and stuff," Tess said. "But I'll clean up first."

"Me, too," Tyler said.

Once in her room, Tess pulled off her mother's sweater. The big purple stain was a bruise on the light yarn. Tess dug through her drawers until she found something cozy, pulled on a sweatshirt, and opened her history book. Who could concentrate? Instead, she turned on the computer and waited to log into her diary.

Dear Diary, she wrote. *How are you?*

Tess stopped, listening to the soothing electric hum of the computer. Wasn't it sort of weird to ask a computer how it was? Like it had any feelings. And asking a diary things was sort of babyish, too. Like it could help her. She thought for a minute, and a great idea came to her. How about writing to God? After all, he had feelings, and she could ask him things, too. Not a bad plan. She moved the backspace bar to erase the first five words and rewrote them.

Dear God,

How are you? There, that was better. *I am not doing fine. Not at all. Yesterday Solomon got sick with something and fell, and he is really bad. He might not live. The worst part is how sad Erin is. She is trying to be brave, but I know she has ridden Solomon all her life, and she loves him a lot. Please don't let him die. Also,*

I did go to church today. I liked the singing, but I felt sort of strange. I didn't know anyone, and I couldn't follow the teacher too well. Plus, I feel as if I'm butting in on Erin's church friends. None of them is her Secret Sister, though.

Tess stopped writing for a minute and reached into her pants pocket, pulling out the pack of gum. She carefully unwrapped a piece and licked the powder off the surface before popping the gum into her mouth. She smiled at the thought of Erin chewing her gum, too.

Might as well talk about the really scary part. It wasn't as if God didn't already know.

But worst of all, something horrible is happening to Mom. She fainted this afternoon, and she's been really crabby. Her face is all white. Please, God, don't let anything bad happen to my mom. Please make her well. I know you can. Thank you.

Love, Tess

five

Trust Me

Monday, November 18

"Good morning, class." Ms. Martinez smiled out over the sixth-grade classroom, signaling with her words that the day was about to begin. "Will you please take your seats?"

A beam of light caught Tess's eye. It was a reflection from the two silver lizards with polished turquoise eyes that snapped together to form a hair clip holding back Ms. M.'s long black hair.

"I think she's prettier since she got engaged," Erin whispered to Tess.

Tess nodded her agreement as they sat down next to each other. Ms. M.'s tawny skin was warmed with a slight pink, blushing like the dawn sky just before the sun rises above the horizon. She was going to be married next April.

"When I checked my box in the office this morning, I found a confirmation for our trip this Thursday. Has everyone remembered to get his or her permission slip signed?" Several students groaned, and Ms. M. handed out extra slips. "Anyone who forgets his slip will remain at school with Mrs. Froget's class while the rest of us explore the planetarium in Tucson. So please, get them signed."

After a boring, humdrum lesson on corn pollination, the class split into groups to prepare for the Thanksgiving program. Tess and Erin partnered with Scott Shearin, one of the class clowns, and Bill Adams, his best friend.

"Why did you pick them?" Tess complained to Erin as the two of them went to pick out some costumes from the scrap box. "Bill is disgusting. He's always sucking on his sweatshirt cuffs. If he sits next to me, the spit will get on my clothes."

"Well, Scott is okay," Erin's eyes twinkled as she whispered back. "And we had to pair up boy-girl, Ms. M. said. Don't worry about Bill. He never sits close to anyone."

The four of them gathered around two desks pushed together to make a small table. "I have an idea," Bill offered. "How about we be Indians who massacre the settlers?" His red hair was cropped short all over, and one eyebrow rose while the other stayed where it was. Tess felt cross-eyed trying to focus on both eyebrows at the same time.

"Don't be silly. Hardly any Indians massacred people," Tess shot back. "If anything, we should be the Indians who provided food for the starving pilgrims."

Erin looked at her in surprise. Tess knew she was being crabby but couldn't help it. Her mind was preoccupied with thoughts of her mother, who hadn't even gotten out of bed this morning to kiss Tess good-bye.

"Well, how about being pilgrims, then?" Scott asked. "Erin ought to know about that. She's so religious."

"So what about it?" Tess challenged.

"It's okay," Erin said. "Maybe it's a good idea. What should we do our part of the program on?"

"I don't know. I was just making a suggestion. Tess, what do you think?" Scott asked in a nice voice, in spite of how she had snapped at him.

Tess softened. "Oh, well, how about if two of us are pilgrims and two of us are Native Americans who bring food for the first Thanksgiving?" The others nodded agreement. "We can even use some of this as part of the first meal together." She held up a handful of the parched corn they had examined in the science section on corn pollination. "Come on, let's see what else we can find." For the next half-hour they scouted food and costumes around the classroom, planning to write their script tomorrow. Before long it was lunchtime.

Once settled into their seats in the cafeteria, Erin asked Tess, "Don't you think it's exciting that we get to paint the murals this year?"

Tess nodded, her mouth full of burrito, and looked around the lunchroom. The block walls had been covered with a smooth, green, ceramic surface, and each year the sixth graders painted a mural on one of the four lunchroom walls. That mural stayed there for four years, until the three other walls were painted. Then the next group of sixth graders painted over that wall.

"I wonder what we'll pick as a theme. I was thinking of running for the committee that decides. Do you know when the elections are?" Tess asked.

"February, I think," Erin answered.

"Sorry I was such a dud this morning," Tess said. "My mom is sick, and I guess I've been thinking about that a lot."

"Oh. Is she okay?" Erin asked, poking a fork into several postage-stamp-sized pieces of lettuce.

"I don't know. She fainted at lunch yesterday. Then she didn't even get up to fix us breakfast today. My dad fixed it, which is really weird. He made us hot cereal but wouldn't let me put any sugar on it."

"Maybe she has the flu."

"Maybe. How's Solomon?"

"Not too good," Erin admitted sadly. "I keep thinking about him. Yesterday my grandma said he couldn't even stand up. The vet is going to come over to check on him tomorrow. He's...he's getting old. I looked up 'founder' on my encyclopedia CD, and it said that Secretariat, a famous race horse, died from founder. I'm worried."

"I'm sorry. This isn't such a good week for us, is it? But the trip on Thursday will be cool! I can't believe our class won the science contest. Of course, we did spend two months and a whole lot of work on it."

"Yeah, well, the volcano idea was good. Even if Joann was bossy the whole time, she was a good team leader. I wish I could have a winning idea, just once. I'm lucky to get my homework done on time," Erin said. "Let's go out and play Trust Me with Joann and Katie." She crumbled the last part of the gluey brownie into her mouth before picking up her tray to take to the lunchroom counter. Tess followed her outside.

"What's Trust Me?" Tess asked.

"Haven't you ever played it? It's really fun. One person is blindfolded, and the others lead her around. Sometimes she has to sit on something, trusting that it's not a big wad of gum or something, or follow after them, trusting that they aren't leading her into a slimy puddle. Then, when you're at the end, you have to guess where you are. Joann asked me this morning if we wanted to play, and I said I'd ask you."

"It sounds okay," Tess agreed. "As long as you're with them! I don't trust everybody, but I trust you."

Tiny yellow leaves blew off one of the few trees outside. Most of the landscaping was red desert rock and gravel with mounds of cacti crouching among them like curled-up hedgehogs. A few wilting white blooms clung to some bushes, like scoops of ice cream dropped among the greenery.

As they headed toward Joann and Katie, Erin said, "I was thinking. For the field trip on Thursday, why don't we do a Secret Sister snack swap?"

"Cool! What's that?" Tess asked.

"Well, you pack snacks in a lunch bag for me, surprising me with things you think I'd like, and I'll do the same for you. That way, when we have our snack on the bus, it will be a surprise."

"Deal!" Tess agreed. As they always did whenever they made a Secret Sister deal, each took off her charm bracelet and switched it with the identical one the other wore. Tess hoped her mother would be well enough to help her shop for snacks. Her dad might insist on nine-grain granola bars, which definitely would not make a fun snack swap.

six

Worse
and Worse

Wednesday, November 20

"You shouldn't drag that thing, or you'll get holes in it," Tess said. Tyler picked his backpack off the ground as they continued to walk home. "I sure hope Mom is feeling better today. At least she got up and made breakfast this morning."

"Yeah, I was worried we'd have to have that whole-wheat glue for breakfast again. Yuck. It jolly well made me sick all day yesterday. And I starved at lunchtime since I couldn't eat a vegetarian sandwich in front of Big Al. He thinks any food that didn't start out on four feet is a waste of time. Except cheese puffs."

"Hey, the garage door is open," Tess said. "And Dad's Jeep is inside. I wonder what he's doing home so early."

The two of them walked through the garage into the laundry room. "I say, Watson," Tyler said, "someone had better do this laundry, or it will take over the house."

The two hampers were heaped full, spilling dirty socks and inside-out T-shirts onto the floor. Their mother's blue sweater was on top of the washing machine with a paste of stain remover hiding the blotch.

"Look, Sherlock Holmes, don't call me Watson. I am not your assistant. I guess Mom didn't feel well enough to do the wash. Maybe I'll do some tonight," Tess said. "Hey! Mom, Dad, anybody home?" She kicked off her shoes before entering the kitchen.

"In here," her father called from the family room. "Come on in."

Tyler grabbed a soda from the refrigerator and popped the top. They walked into the family room. Tess could tell their dad had been rubbing his forehead again, which he did whenever he was upset. It was all red.

"Why are you home so early?" Tyler asked.

"Well, Mom fainted again this morning," their dad said.

"Oh no," Tess cried. "What's happening?"

"We're not sure. I came home, and we went to the doctor. He has a couple of ideas, and he took some of Mom's blood. A couple of years ago Mom had a bad bout with anemia, which is when your blood has too few red cells. It makes you dizzy and weak. Last time, though, the symptoms weren't as strong, so they want to rule out a couple of other things, too. They sent the blood to the lab, and we should have the results next Monday. But until then, we need to let Mom rest and keep up around here ourselves."

"I thought she had the flu," Tyler said hopefully.

"Well, Ty, we all thought so. But she doesn't have a fever; so they've ruled that out. We'll just have to wait."

"I'll help with the laundry," Tess offered.

"Me, too," Tyler said. "And I'd be glad to call for pizza delivery."

"Yeah," Tess agreed, hoping her dad didn't have some vegetable vitamin drink in mind instead.

"All right, Ty." Mr. Thomas tousled Tyler's hair. "Go ahead and call. Then you can come with Tess and me for our hike."

"Boffo!" Tyler ran from the room to grab the phone book and look up the number for Pizza Palace.

"I guess that means we'll do Squaw Peak tonight, huh?" Tess said.

"Yep, I guess so. I know you were looking forward to a tougher hike, but I don't think Ty could keep up."

Tess looked at her hands, picking at another hangnail before speaking again. "What about Mom? Will she be all right?"

"I'll leave my pager number, and she can page me if she needs something. Millie next door will be home, too. I already checked."

"I mean, will she be all right, you know, forever?" Tess asked, dabbing the blood from the hangnail with the corner of her sleeve.

"She'll be okay. Don't worry. We'll get through this to-gether," her dad answered. He smiled with his mouth, but his eyes weren't smiling. They looked tired and red. He was scared, which scared Tess even more. "Why don't you start on the laundry, and I'll finish paying some bills?"

"Okay. Can I say hi to Mom first?"

"Sure. Just don't wake her up if she's sleeping." Her dad rubbed his forehead one last time and turned back to his stack of bills.

Tess slipped from the room and went down the hall to check on her mom. Tiptoeing into her mother's room, Tess looked at her mom's sleeping face. She looked too still, her face sort of yellowish gray. Truly afraid now, Tess backed up and headed into her own room to pray.

Later, as Tess hiked with her dad and Tyler, her brother struggled to keep up. "You guys, wait up," he called as the others huffed up the last switchback before reaching the top of Squaw Peak.

It was almost cold. Although the mountain was in town, it was high, and as the light grew dim, cold settled in the air like an invisible hand pressing down into the warm valley. They sat down on a smooth, cool rock, and each pulled out a water bottle. Scruffy little weeds sprouted from the edge of the summit, wilting in the evening shade but sure to cheer up again in the morning. *Even plants need to rest*, Tess thought.

"What did you guys do in school this week?" Mr. Thomas asked.

"We're making paper out of recycled newsprint," Tyler said. "It makes great spit wads. Can I go look for lizards?"

"Yes, but stay in sight of us," Mr. Thomas said. "I

imagine you haven't done too much, Tess, besides get ready for your field trip tomorrow."

"Well, we're practicing for our Thanksgiving presentation. I'm with Erin, of course." Tess smiled as she pulled a piece of her Secret Sister gum from her pocket. "But also Scott and Bill. Sometimes they drive me crazy. Like Scott said Erin should be a pilgrim since she was so religious." She unwrapped the gum and slipped it into her mouth, letting the burst of cinnamon warm her up from the inside. *Dear Lord,* she prayed inside her head, *please let Solomon get well and help Erin to be happy.*

"She is religious, Tess." Dad answered.

"Well, I like that. Maybe I'm religious, too," she ventured, watching her father's reaction.

"You know, you might want to concentrate on what's happening at home right now and leave that church stuff alone for a while. I'm sure Erin's great, and her family seems really nice, but you have your boots full with school and helping around home."

"Well, what about church next week?" She wasn't even sure she wanted to go, but she asked just in case she did.

"Let's cross that river when we come to the bank," he said. "Do you need anything for the field trip?"

"Well, I need to make a snack bag. And you need to sign my permission form."

"We can stop at Smitty's on the way home to buy snacks, and I'll sign the sheet before bed. Just remind me."

"Okay." Tess hugged him and sighed with relief. Smitty's would have good snack possibilities. She didn't want her sister's bag to be a dud.

"Now, we had better get a move on." Jim Thomas stood up and waved to Tyler.

"Boffo!" Tyler called from a few yards away. "I found a friend for Hercules."

Her dad ambled over to look at the lizard, but Tess stayed put. *Great. Just what we need. Another ugly reptile around the house.*

Crummy 8 Ball

Thursday Morning, November 21

"Okay, class, please load the bus," Mr. Twiddle, the principal, called out through his megaphone. His suspenders held up a pressed pair of navy blue pants. As usual, his clothes were neatly in order, just the way he kept the school.

"What are we supposed to load it with?" someone said with a snicker, but they all clambered on, trying to grab seats near the back. The dandelion-yellow bus had the words "Scottsdale Unified School District Number 10" painted on the side.

About halfway back Tess and Erin snagged a good seat with an open window right behind Joann and Katie. Joann's shiny black cornrows were pulled back into a ponytail this morning, her amber skin softly reflecting the morning light.

"Yeah, you guys, sit behind us," she said as Tess and Erin scooted in.

"Good," Katie added, her brown eyes smiling from below her visor. "I don't trust any of them." She jerked her finger toward the back where most of the boys were. "I heard one of them say they have an egg-peg bag."

"What's an egg-peg bag?" Tess asked.

"It's a bag of raw eggs they throw out the window," Erin said. "Someone in my brother's class got in big trouble for that last year."

"They only get in trouble if they're caught," Katie said.

"Well, I'm not watching. I have enough trouble of my own. Did you bring my snack bag?" Tess asked Erin.

"Yep, I did. Did you bring mine?"

"Yep. Let's switch." Tess handed Erin a brown paper lunch bag that she had decorated with markers, and Erin handed Tess one she had painted with watercolors.

"Yours looks great!" Tess said. "I didn't know you could paint." She marveled at the brown bag on which Erin had painted two fluffy kittens playing with a bright red yarn ball. The names "Erin and Tess" were written above the cats. "Did you paint the names, too?"

Erin nodded. "Well, I draw a little." She blushed. "I copied the picture from some stationery my grandma gave me for my birthday last year. Since I'm not so smart, I guess art is one thing I can do."

"Stop saying that! You are smart. I think you should run for the mural committee, not me," Tess said. "What did you put in here?" She rummaged through the bag, smiling at all the thoughtful things Erin had packed.

"I packed Lemon Heads, of course," Erin said.

"Of course!" Tess giggled. Lemon Heads were the best. Tess dug through and found wax bottle candies, barbecue potato chips, and a sports drink.

"What are you guys doing?" Joann interrupted.

"We packed a snack bag for each other." Tess looked at Erin, and Erin nodded to her. "We're Secret Sisters," Tess continued.

"What's that?" Katie asked, her round face flushed from the heat of her too-warm jacket. She unzipped it, pulled it off, and stuffed it into the space between Joann and herself.

"Well, since Erin and I only have brothers," Tess said, "we decided to be sisters to each other. You know, sharing clothes, giving advice, doing stuff together. Like real sisters would. Only we don't tell too many people. So keep it quiet, okay?"

"We won't tell," Joann said. She looked at Katie before continuing. "Would you guys mind if we copied you? I mean, if we didn't tell anyone?"

"It's okay," Erin said. "Maybe we could share ideas sometime." Katie and Joann nodded before turning around in their seats to face front again, leaving Tess and Erin with some privacy.

"How's Solomon?" Tess asked.

"Um, not good." Erin's answer was muffled as she bit into an apple. She had a major appetite all the time, yet she was skinny. Tess looked at her friend's thin cheeks, which were partially hidden by her caramel-blond hair, and wondered how anyone could eat so much and weigh so little. "Dr. Wenzel said Solomon should be getting better by now, but he's not. My grandpa is really upset. Said he might as well sell the ranch if the horses are going to die. Which I know he doesn't want to do."

"Well, you're not sure Solomon's going to die, are you?" Tess asked.

"No, not really. I'm worried though. Solomon has always been closest to me, and me to him. I don't know what I'll do if we lose him." She swallowed before asking, "What about your mom?"

"She's not going to die!" Tess practically shouted. "My dad said so."

"No, silly, I meant how is she." Erin patted her friend's shoulder softly. "I know she's not going to die."

"Sorry I yelled at you. I guess I'm afraid. She went to the doctor yesterday, and they are doing some tests. The results will be back Monday. They told us they think it might be anemia, which she had once before. But she never got this sick last time she had it. Tyler and I think it's cancer. Her dad, my grandpa, died from that, you know."

"I'm so sorry. I've been praying for you every time I chew my gum," Erin said.

"Me, too." Tess smiled.

The bus jerked as the driver shifted the gears to stop at a traffic light. Tess couldn't be sure, but she thought she smelled rotten tomatoes. *Crazy! Must be something outside.*

"Did you tell your parents you asked Jesus into your life?" Erin asked, finishing the apple.

"Um, no. With everything going on, you know, the time just never seems right."

"Well, you're going to have to tell them, Tess. I know it's hard, but it's the right thing to do."

"I know. I will."

They sat in silence for a minute until Katie leaned over the seat. "Guess what I brought."

"What?" Erin asked.

Katie stuck her hand into her backpack and pulled out a round, black, plastic ball. "A Magic 8 Ball. Want to play?"

Erin looked uncomfortable. "I don't know. I don't think so, huh, Tess?"

"Um, right," Tess answered. But Katie didn't turn back around.

"Why not? Aren't you guys curious about anything?"

"Yeah, but we're busy," Tess answered. She glanced over at Erin, who looked uneasy.

Katie was about to protest when she blurted out, "Oh no! Look at that!" They all turned to see Kenny and Russell throwing tomatoes and an egg out the window. They hit their target, an open convertible parked by the side of the road. Rotten tomato meat splattered all over the snowy white upholstery, and the egg streaked across the hood, a messy guided missile. Laughing, the boys turned back around.

"What should we do?" Joann whispered. "Tell?"

Erin and Tess sat there, stunned, as Katie piped in. "I don't know. Let's ask the Magic 8 Ball." She shook the ball a little bit, asking it, "Should we tell?"

"What does it say?" Tess asked, curious and a little tense. Erin turned her head away, not wanting to see, Tess guessed.

"It says, 'My sources say no,'" Katie replied.

"Well, I don't know. Maybe we should tell," Tess said.

"Let's wait awhile and ask it again," Joann suggested. "Do you guys have a question? How about your horse, Erin?"

"You guys don't really think a Magic 8 Ball has answers, do you?" Erin said.

"Maybe. Who knows?" Katie shrugged.

Before Erin could protest, Katie asked, "Will Erin's horse get better?" and shook the Magic 8 Ball. Then she read aloud, "'Yes, definitely.' See? I told you. Now don't you feel better?"

Erin didn't say anything, but Tess thought she smiled a bit.

"How about if my mom will get well?" Tess asked. She felt a queasy sensation in her stomach as if a soggy sponge was sitting in there. Somehow, she knew it was wrong to ask. But she really wanted to know.

"I didn't know your mom was sick," Joann said, looking concerned.

"It's probably nothing," Tess answered, but she didn't look at Joann.

Katie shook the ball and asked, "Will Tess's mom get better?"

"What does it say?" Tess asked.

"Reply hazy, try again," Katie answered. She shook the ball again, and asked, "Will Tess's mom get better?" She frowned as she read the answer, "Don't count on it."

eight

Star Dust

Thursday Afternoon, November 21

The Magic 8 Ball's answer about Tess's mom wasn't a great way to begin the field trip. As soon as they arrived at the planetarium, Tess put her worries behind her, telling herself the ball was only a game. But thoughts about her mom nagged her.

"Please stay with your three buddies," Ms. M. called out. "We'll all meet at the Sky Theater for the movie *The Comets Are Coming* in two hours. Then we're off to lunch." With that she pulled her tan explorer's cap over her shiny black hair and led the way into the planetarium.

"Where should we go first?" Erin asked, as she, Tess, Joann, and Katie linked arms.

"Let's follow the outline on the map they sent us," Joann suggested.

Tess raised her eyebrows at Erin and tried to stifle a giggle. Joann always played by the rules.

"Okay," Katie agreed, and they followed Joann to the meteor shower exhibit.

Hundreds of long-stemmed lights hung from the ceiling, their tiny heads capped with bright, pinkish-white bulbs. They scattered their radiance all over the dark blue walls on which filmy clouds and majestic, pinwheeled galaxies rolled through a painted universe.

Once inside the room displaying meteors and asteroid pieces that had fallen to Earth, Tess knew for sure she loved science. Glowing gases and pulsating stars surrounded her, reminding her how big the universe was and of the One who had created it.

"Do you guys want to go to the solar system exhibit?" Joann asked a few minutes later. She was actually asking instead of telling. Tess couldn't believe it.

"Sure," she agreed, and the others followed along.

"Well," Joann said once they reached the exhibit, "we have to complete one experiment while we're here. We'd like to do the planet pendulum, right, Katie?" She looked over at Katie, who almost always agreed. Tess wondered if Katie was such an airhead when Joann wasn't around.

"I want to make my own comet. How about you?" Tess asked Erin.

"Sounds good," Erin agreed. "Since it's just the next station over, I don't think it'll matter if we do different ones." She and Tess walked over to the comet station.

"It says we have to wear these geeky gloves," Tess said, picking up the black rubber pair between thumb and forefinger. "I hope the last person who wore these didn't have some disease!" She stretched out her fingers and slipped each hand into a glove. Erin did the same. Two girls from another school came up behind them, impatient for their turn.

"Something smells," one of them said to the other, looking at Erin and Tess.

"It's not me. I showered today. Maybe it's the experiment. Or someone else," the second girl said in a snide voice. Tess knew she shouldn't let it get to her, but the remark made her mad. She wasn't going to be bullied out of making a comet, no matter what the girls said. She grabbed a chunk of dry ice and handed it to Erin.

"Here, we're supposed to put this in a plastic bag and chop it with this hammer until we have two cups worth of chips." She looked back at the other girls before continuing. "It might take a *long* time." As she turned back to mix some corn syrup and sand together in the large plastic bowl, she saw the new girls leaving. Good.

Fifteen minutes later they had smashed together a snowball of dry ice, water, sand, corn syrup, and ammonia. Their comet was smoking. "Good job!" the planetarium employee said. "Would you like a Polaroid picture? I can give you each one for one dollar." The girls agreed, then went back to the planet pendulum to pick up Katie and Joann.

Their time flew by quickly, and the girls spent a few minutes in the gift shop before heading into the Sky Theater for the show. Quiet music gently filled the room, like soft mist on a foggy night. A faint fragrance of incense rose from hidden dispensers behind the walls, scattering orange and ginger scents throughout the theater. It seemed almost like a church.

"Where should we sit?" Katie whispered. They had entered through heavy black doors and were amazed that the entire room was shaped like an overturned half of a large, creamy white egg. The seats were under the shell.

"How about over there?" Erin, bold for once, led them to four seats next to Scott Shearin and his buddy group.

"Why do you want to sit next to them?" Joann asked, huffy again.

Tess looked at Erin and smiled. Tess's suspicions were confirmed: Erin liked Scott.

"Check these out!" Tess whispered, fingering the smooth brass plates screwed into the wooden armrests between the seats. The plates named financial donors to the theater. "Whose name is on yours? Mine says Jacqueline Fisherman."

Erin leaned over to read hers. "Mine says Vivian Cheeseball!" They both broke out in giggles, feeling sorry for poor old Vivian.

"I wouldn't marry anyone whose last name was Cheeseball!" Tess laughed.

"What's that? You're going to marry a cheese ball?" Scott interrupted, and Tess blushed. Erin gave her a warning look, though, and Tess didn't say anything back at Scott for her Secret Sister's sake.

Instead Tess leaned over and teased Erin, "Don't try to hold his hand in the dark now." Erin poked her in the ribs and pointed to the center of the theater.

Russell and Kenny stood in front of the major projector, which was on a platform in the middle of the room. Kenny held up his hands and made rabbit ears in front of the light, projecting it a hundred times larger onto the walls. Everyone laughed as he did a dog, a snake, and a cat. Flushed from the attention, he leaned too hard against the projector, and the room gasped in shock as the projector wobbled, then almost toppled off the platform. A loud voice boomed, "Would the class clown please take his seat so the movie can begin?" Kenny grew radish red and took his seat, with Russell tagging along behind.

Suddenly the room was dark, and thousands of stars appeared on the 360-degree screen overhead, like grains of electric salt spilled onto midnight blue velvet. Tess leaned back in her reclining seat and listened to the narrator explain a star's birth.

"Awesome," she heard Scott whisper to his buddy as a spectacular head-on collision between a galaxy and an intruder sent out ripples of energy that triggered the birth of a new star. Eventually the stars die out, the movie explained, extinct forever.

Gazing at the stars and sucking a Lemon Head, Tess wondered at the power it must take to make all those millions of stars and to create planets. How very small Earth seemed next to it all. A few minutes later, after the blowtorch tails of several comets blazed across the sky, the lights slowly came up, and Ms. M. herded them all to the bus. They were on their way to McDonald's.

"I don't know why we couldn't order for ourselves," Joann complained twenty minutes later, as she bit into a cheeseburger.

"Probably because the school had to pay for us," Katie answered. "Hey, Tess, don't sit there! A big wad of gum is on the seat."

"Thanks." Tess sat at the next table, saving a space for Erin. "At least they didn't order us Happy Meals."

"Really." Joann plucked the pickle out of her burger and flung it onto the wrapper. "Anyone want my pickle?"

"Uh, no thanks," Katie answered.

"What did you guys think of the planetarium?" Joann asked between bites.

"I really liked it. Especially the stars. And star dust," Tess answered.

"Did you guys know the horoscope part of the paper is called Star Dust?" Joann asked.

"Yes. I...I used to read it," Tess admitted. "Stupid, huh?"

"No, it's not stupid!" Katie protested. "I read it. I was looking for the astrology stuff in the exhibit."

"Astrology is not the same as astronomy," Joann instructed Katie. "Astronomy is about stars and the planets and stuff—the science. Astrology is about goofy horoscopes." She dunked a mop of fries into her ketchup and popped them into her mouth.

"I used to think horoscopes were true, too," Tess spoke up again. "But didn't you see that about stars? They are born and live and die, just like people. How can they be gods and know the future?"

"I don't know," Katie admitted. She thought about it. "It's as good as anything else though."

"Actually, I feel more and more sure that there is a real God after watching that," Tess said. "It couldn't have all happened by accident."

"Maybe you're right," Joann admitted. She waved her hand in the air to flag down Erin, who had just picked up her lunch and was aiming toward them. Then Joann stuffed some more fries in her mouth and slurped it all down with an orange drink. "I don't feel so good. Maybe I'll stop eating." She pushed back the tray. "Look at Kenny and Russell." She frowned in disapproval.

Tess glanced out the window and shook her head. Kenny and Russell were swimming in the baby ball pit. Hopeless.

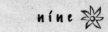

nine

Busted

Thursday Evening, November 21

"Remain seated, class," Ms. M. called toward the back of the bus. Although everyone was worn out from the day, you would never have known it from the noise level on the bus.

"Hey, want to ask the Magic 8 Ball some more questions?" Katie turned toward Tess and Erin. "I could ask about boys or something, if you want."

"No, thanks," Tess said uncomfortably. "We're talking."

Erin slurped another Gummy Worm into her mouth but nodded her agreement. She stuck a Gummy Worm on each of her two front teeth and grinned at Tess.

"You're so goofy," Tess teased.

"Okay, then," Katie said, leaning across the aisle to someone else. "You guys want to ask the Magic 8 Ball some questions?" Having found someone else who wanted to play, she left Erin and Tess alone.

Tess sucked on Lemon Heads, biting through their tangy coating before finding the smooth, sweet center. She looked out the window and watched the lonely tumbleweeds roll across the highway, east to west and back again, never content.

"What are you thinking?" Erin asked.

"About my mom. About stars and astrology. I used to read my horoscope, you know," Tess said.

"Really? Why?"

"Well, I wanted to know what was going to happen. I still do. Same thing with the Magic 8 Ball. Sometimes not knowing what's going to happen makes me scared, like with my mom."

"I know what you mean. Like Solomon, too. Although it's not as serious as with your mom," Erin finished, slipping another worm into her mouth.

"That's why I let Katie ask the Magic 8 Ball about Mom. But even when Katie was doing it, I felt bad. I . . . I think I knew it was wrong."

Erin blushed. "I was glad to hear that about Solomon, too. But the Bible says talking to psychics and other magic stuff, like Magic 8 Balls and horoscopes, is sin. My Aunt Ginny explained that to me last year when the psychic line advertisement came on TV."

"So what should I do? Am I not a Christian anymore?" Tess popped another Lemon Head into her mouth, scraping the candy against her molar. *Ouch! Hope that isn't a cavity!*

"No, silly. Once you're a Christian you're always a

Christian. You're still going to have problems and make mistakes. Just ask God to forgive you when you do, and poof! it's gone." Erin giggled. "Remember, as far as east is from west."

Tess closed her eyes to pray and confess her sin. She was just finishing when she heard a great splat. "What was that?" she asked, her eyes flying open.

"My 8 Ball! My 8 Ball! It's busted," Katie moaned.

Erin leaned over so Tess could see into the aisle, and sure enough, the black ball lay shattered in pieces, its purple dye running down the bus floorboards. "So much for magic," Erin whispered to Tess.

"I know. Doesn't seem real powerful," Tess giggled.

A couple of minutes later the steady humming of the bus engine was punctured by a sharp call. "Ms. Martinez, Ms. Martinez, please stop the bus. Joann has to throw up!" Katie called, helping Joann stand up and shakily make her way to the front of the bus.

Everyone grew quiet and watched. The driver steered the big yellow bus to the side of the road, and Joann practically leaped out. She leaned over into a dusty gulch and lost her lunch while everyone else stared out the window.

"Do you have to stare?" Tess shouted at Russell and Kenny, who were making barfing noises.

"Hey, want a fresh egg?" Russell threatened her, holding up his egg-peg bag as Tess turned around.

"We should have told on them. They need it," she whispered.

A minute later Joann slumped back onto the bus, keeping her head down in embarrassment. Katie put her arm around Joann as she sat down.

Tess leaned forward. "Don't worry. You'll be okay. Everyone barfs at a bad time. Once I barfed strawberry milk all over the lady next to me at a piano recital." Joann smiled weakly, then leaned her head against the bus's window. Tess was surprised at how much she cared about Joann's feelings. Ever since the time Joann organized the class to make a card for Tess when she burned her hand, Tess looked at her a little differently.

An hour later the bus pulled into the Coronado Elementary School parking lot. The street lamps were beginning to flicker on, then off again. It was not quite nighttime but no longer daytime either. The few cars scattered throughout the oversized parking lot looked like scraps of confetti left over from a surprise party. Tess eagerly looked out the window, searching for her mom and dad. Secretly she hoped her mom was well enough to come pick her up. She had so much to tell her.

"Isn't that Principal Twiddle?" Erin whispered. "And two police officers."

The men approached the bus, and everyone stayed seated, though no one had told them to do that.

The bus driver cranked open the doors, and Ms. M. walked down the steps to talk with the men. A minute later a burly policeman climbed into the bus and said, "Earlier today a very angry man called the police station to report that someone had vandalized his brand-new automobile with rotten tomatoes and eggs. These allegedly were thrown out of this very bus. Luckily a bystander wrote down the bus number and called the district. Now, I have all night, but I'll venture some of your parents might start getting anxious if we're on this bus too long. So no one is leaving this bus until the guilty party comes forward." Leaning against the rail beside the driver, the policeman moved one hand to his revolver holster. All eyes were on it.

The silence in the bus was so heavy it could crush stones. For a minute or two, no one said anything, and the police officer waited patiently. Finally Russell stood up and looked menacingly at Kenny, who stood up after him.

Tess whispered to Erin, "Looks like the 8 Ball isn't the only thing busted on this trip."

Tess looked out the window and saw Russell's dad. *Boy, oh boy, what he doesn't know.* But he would know real soon. Russell and Kenny followed the officer down the bus stairs. Silently the rest of the sixth graders picked up their belongings and followed behind.

ten

The Stars and the Whole World

Thursday Night, November 21

"Hi, honey!" Tess's mom called from the couch in the family room. Her wool slippers cuddled her feet, and she had a plaid flannel blanket draped across her shoulders. "Did you have a good time?"

"Yes, I really did. How are you, Mom?"

"I'm okay. Tell me about your trip."

"You can't believe it. We saw a movie in 3-D on comets and learned about the life cycle of stars and other science stuff. It was great. And a guy who worked there took a picture of Erin and me making our own comet. Here's mine."

"Well, don't you look like a real scientist," said her mom as she studied the photo.

"Did you get me anything?" Tyler asked, lugging Hercules into the family room.

"Yep." Tess fished a small bag out of her backpack. "These are glow-in-the-dark stars for your bedroom ceiling. If you leave the lights on for a couple of hours after you put them up, they'll glow in the dark until you fall asleep. I got myself a pack, too."

"Cool! I'll put them up right now," Tyler said. "How was the bus ride?"

"All right." Tess sat next to her mom and snuggled under the blanket with her. "Except Kenny and Russell pitched rotten tomatoes and raw eggs out the window. When we got back to the school, the police were waiting for them. I think they're in big, big trouble."

"Good," Tyler said. "Kenny bushed Big Al a couple of weeks ago."

"What's bushing?" Mrs. Thomas asked.

"It's when a big kid picks up a little kid and shoves him in a bush," Tyler explained.

"How mean!" their mom said.

"Ta ta, I'm going to put up the stars." Tyler toted his horned toad with him; Hercules glared out of the side of his cage, his spiked neck bristling under his rough brown skin.

"How are you feeling, Mom?" Tess asked, drawing closer to her mother's warmth.

"A little better, honey. Not as tired tonight. I'll be glad when we get back those test results."

"Me, too. Um, don't we have a Bible around here?"

"Gee, Tess, I'm not sure. We used to have my dad's old one around here somewhere, but I haven't seen it in forever. Check under the TV cabinet."

Tess slid off the couch and crawled over to the cabinet, pulling open the latch.

"Gross!" she exclaimed as a fat, tan cricket leaped out at her. "Dad! Dad! Kill the cricket," she called out toward the kitchen as she jumped back onto the couch.

"Aw, it's just a little cricket. It's not going to hurt you," her dad said as he strolled in.

"I don't care if it's going to hurt me or not. It's disgusting. Please get it," Tess replied.

One of the troubles with living in the desert was the bugs. Once, when the family still lived at their old house, Tess woke up in the middle of the night to find a scorpion crawling on her pillow. There had been construction nearby, and it had upset the scorpion's habitat. She slept in her mom and dad's room for a couple of nights after that.

"There." Mr. Thomas scooped up the cricket between two pieces of newspaper and walked toward Tyler's room. "Hercules is in for a special treat."

Tess moved back to the cabinet and, after a little digging, found the huge, leather-bound Bible that had "Patrick O'Connor" engraved on the cover.

"Is this it, Mom?" she asked.

"Yes. My, doesn't that bring back memories." Her eyes grew soft. "My dad read that every morning. Grandma Kate wasn't much for Bible reading, but my dad, Grandpa Pat, was."

"Can I take it to my room?"

"Sure. Be careful with it though."

"I will." Tess gave her mom a little peck on the cheek before walking to her room. Once there, she flipped the light switch which turned on her radio, not the lights.

Smiling, she remembered asking her father to rig her switch. A girl has priorities, after all.

Flopping down on the bed, she licked her finger and began to turn page after page of the thin paper. It crackled with age, and the gold gilt on the edges was almost completely worn off. A musty smell wafted from the book as she gently flipped through it. But the smell was sweet, too, like a slightly dusty rose. After several minutes of paging through, she was about to give up when she saw black ink scrawls in the margin of a page. She stopped and read the passage that was underlined, Psalm 56:3-4. There was a date next to it: March 13. *Hmm. What could that mean?*

She was interrupted by a slight knock on the door. "Who is it?" she called out, letting the Bible close.

"Me," Tyler called back.

"Come in."

"Thanks for the stars. Do you want me to help you put up yours? I finished mine. I handed Dad the stars, and he stuck them on my ceiling. I could hand them to you, and you could probably reach if you stood on your bed."

"All right," Tess agreed. She pointed at Hercules. "Why are you carrying him around with you tonight?" Usually he stayed in Tyler's room.

"I don't know," Tyler shrugged. "He makes me feel better, I guess."

"Are you worried about Mom?"

"Yeah."

"Me, too," Tess admitted. "She says she feels better, but she doesn't look too well."

"I know. I'm worried she's going to die."

"Don't be silly, Tyler. She'll be okay. It's probably the anemia."

"Grandpa Pat died though. Maybe she has the same cancer that killed him," Tyler said.

"Maybe," Tess said, glancing at the Bible on the bed. The thought made her stomach fill with acid. "Let's put up the stars."

A couple of hours later, after dinner and some quick homework, Tess slipped into a pair of soft pajamas and turned on her computer. The room was dark, except for the soft light of the computer monitor and the twinkling majesty of the stars shining down from her ceiling.

"Star light, star bright, first star I see tonight, I wish I may I wish I might that Mom would get better tonight," Tess whispered softly before logging into her diary.

> *Dear God,*
>
> *How are you? I am fine, I think. We had a really great trip to the planetarium today. It was so fun, and I feel like I learned a lot. Except that Kenny and Russell got in trouble (but they deserved it). Also, Joann got sick. Do you remember Joann? We played Trust Me with her and Katie last week. I did trust them, and Erin, too.*

Tess sat there for a minute before continuing.

> *I'm worried about Mom. We played Magic 8 Ball, and even though I don't believe in that, I think she might die.*

She stopped writing again and glanced up at the ceiling, aflame with neon yellow stars.

Tess asked herself, *If God can make the stars and the whole world, can I trust him to take care of Mom?* Then she tapped out some more thoughts into her computer.

I guess it is sort of like playing Trust Me with you, Lord. But it seems a lot easier to trust someone with something little like a game. This is my mom, and it's a lot harder to trust. I guess I need to though. I said I had faith, and I do. I think it's about time I told my parents I'm a Christian. I'll tell them tomorrow, even though I'm a little scared. Please take care of Mom, Jesus. Fix her. Thank you for all the stars and everything else that you made and take care of.

Love, Tess

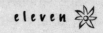

eleven

Try and
Try Again

Friday, November 22

As soon as Erin walked into the classroom, Tess knew something was wrong. Erin's face was puffy, and red splotches dotted her face. She sat down at her desk and folded her hands on top of each other.

"What's the matter?" Tess whispered just before the Pledge of Allegiance.

"He's going to die," she whispered back, tears sliding down her cheeks.

"What? Who is?" Tess asked, really concerned now.

"I'll write you a note." Erin sniffed. She took out a scrap of paper and scribbled quickly before passing it across the aisle to Tess.

She read, "Solomon got worse, and they're going to put him down today."

Tess turned the paper over and wrote, "What does 'down' mean? I thought he was already resting."

Erin bit her lip, and Tess could see tears brimming in her eyes. "No, that means they are going to put him to sleep. He'll die today."

Oh, no. This was bad. Tess reached across the aisle and squeezed her friend's arm to tell her how much she cared. Then she wrote, "I'm so sorry, Sis. I really am," and passed the note back across the aisle. What else could she say? Tess tried hard not to let Erin see her own tears, but they were there. Solomon had seemed like her pet, too.

The morning dragged by until finally it was recess. They hung out alone. Joann wasn't in school today, and Katie played with someone else.

"I brought you something. It's in my locker. Remind me to give it to you before you leave today." Erin picked at the seam of her jeans.

"Okay," Tess said. "I'm really sorry about Solomon. I know how much he means to you."

"Yeah, he's the only pet I really ever had. Our dog, Butch, is my brother's. Last year I wanted a cat, but Mom said one baby animal at a time was enough. I don't want to think about it anymore. Do you want to jump rope?"

"Okay," Tess agreed, and that's what they did until class started again.

After school, Tyler and Tess scrounged around the kitchen, looking for snacks.

"I sure wish Mom would get better. There's nothing to eat in the house, and I don't trust what Dad would buy."

Tyler dug through the cupboards. He finally zeroed in on a half-empty bag of chips and pulled them out from the back of the pantry.

"Say, old girl, what's that?" He pointed at the pretty floral package Tess had set on the kitchen table.

"A present from Erin. I guess I should open it, huh? She wanted me to wait until I got home." Tess slit through the tape on the side just as her mother and father came into the room.

"Look! A Bible! And it has a blue-jeans cover with pockets, just like Erin's. Isn't it cool?" Tess pulled out a red pen and a black pen and some Passion Fruit lip gloss from the back pocket. She smiled. Of course her Secret Sister would remember her favorite flavor of lip gloss.

Mr. Thomas cleared his throat, and Tess looked up. "What's the matter?" she asked, catching the odd look on her dad's face.

"I don't know about all this religious stuff, Tess. I mean, maybe you're going overboard here."

"Well, I—I like it. I decided . . ." Tess swallowed hard before continuing, feeling a little lightheaded. "I decided to be a Christian. Last month."

Mr. Thomas stood there for a long minute before walking toward Tess. "Let's sit down," he said, pulling up a chair next to her.

"We're all Christians, Tess. What do you mean you 'decided' to become a Christian?"

"I don't mean just saying I'm a Christian like when we go to church once in a while with Grandma and Grandpa

Thomas, or not being Jewish or Muslim or something. I mean I decided to really learn about Jesus and trust him. All the time. I asked him to forgive my sins, and I am sure he did. That's how I became a Christian," Tess explained, surprised at how calm her voice sounded.

"I know other people in our family read the Bible, 'cause I found Grandpa Pat's last night," she went on. "I know he read it, too, because he underlined a passage and marked a date next to it. March 13. What does that mean, Mom?" Tess turned to face her mother.

"Oh . . . ," her mother's voice trailed off as she sat down, too.

Tyler just stood there with his mouth open, looking like Hercules did when he expected a squirming bug to drop in. Tess didn't know why, but it annoyed her. She decided not to say anything though.

"Well," her mother said, "that's the day my dad learned he had cancer. And a few months later he died." Her eyes filled with tears, and everyone was quiet.

Way to go, Tess, she thought. *Mom was finally feeling better, and you go and make her cry.* Everyone she cared about was crying today.

"I'm sorry, Mom." Tess ran to get her a tissue.

"It's okay, honey. And you're right, my dad did read his Bible. We never did after he died, so I'd forgotten about it until you dug it out last night. And then to know he marked in it when he found out he was sick, well, it touched me. Anyway, I guess I don't see anything wrong with your reading the Bible and going to church, as long as you keep up your schoolwork and other things around here. If Dad says it's okay, that is." Mrs. Thomas blew her nose and looked at her husband.

"I guess so," Mr. Thomas said, an uneasy look on his face. Tess figured he didn't want to upset her mother further. "Just don't get too crazy."

"I won't!" Tess slicked some gloss over her lips. "Hey! How about I make dinner?" she offered. No one said anything, but at least Tyler closed his mouth.

"Not fried chicken." She laughed, remembering how, last month, she had fried her hand instead of the chicken. Her dad ruffled her hair and everyone laughed with her.

"Okay, how about something like sandwiches?" Mr. Thomas suggested. "Then we'll go on a hike, just you and me."

"You've got a deal, Dad," Tess said, as she left the kitchen to change clothes. She remembered about Solomon. She would have to call Erin to see how she was doing and to thank her for the Bible.

twelve

The Sniffer

Sunday Morning, November 24

Tess fingered the blue-jeans cover of her Bible as she waited for Erin to pick her up for church. After just a minute the Janssens pulled up.

"I'm going. See you later," she called down the hall.

"Bye, honey," her mom responded from the kitchen as she turned the page of the newspaper. Her mom still couldn't eat anything in the morning without getting sick, but at least she was out of bed.

Erin's older brother, Tom, was in the car, Tess noted with delight.

"Here, I'll move over." The lightly cinnamon scent of his skin floated over to her as he moved to make room for her in the backseat. And he smiled his megawatt smile. Tess smiled back, catching Erin's wink from the front seat.

"I see you have your new Bible," Erin said over her shoulder.

"Yep, ready to go." Tess felt better having a Bible like everyone else in the Sunday school class. Plus, this week she would know a few of the songs. Still, last night she had prayed that she wouldn't feel too out of place.

She didn't know whether or not to say anything about Solomon. Everyone seemed a little quieter than usual, but at least Erin was smiling. Tess didn't want to mess it up by mentioning the horse. She decided to talk with Erin more privately tomorrow in school.

A few minutes later they arrived. Erin and Tess milled about the class before it started. About halfway through the class a round, happy-faced woman approached the redheaded girl sitting on Erin's other side. The woman whispered something in the girl's ear, who turned and whispered something to Erin. Erin shook her head no and asked Tess, "Do you want to work in the nursery? They need help."

Tess nodded yes. She loved kids.

As Tess slipped out of the class with the other girl, Erin whispered, "I'll come by after class to pick you up."

Once out in the hall the other girl introduced herself. "I'm Melissa. That's my mom who came to get us. She's in charge of the nursery. You're new, aren't you?" Her smile lit up the gray hallway, and Tess felt warmth from her.

"Yes. My name is Tess. I came here with Erin. My, um, family doesn't go here." She wondered for a minute if that was okay. Maybe they wanted only people whose families attended church to work in the nursery. She would be so embarrassed if she had to walk back into the class now.

"Oh." Melissa smiled. It didn't seem to matter. "We're going to do toddlers. Is that okay?"

"Sure. I love kids." They arrived at the doorway and, once inside, kicked off their shoes. Almost immediately a tiny blonde girl wobbled toward Tess.

"Uppy. Uppy." The toddler held her hands toward Tess, who picked her up. Babies smelled so good, like powder and springtime.

"Let's play Ring Around the Rosie." Tess put the little girl down, and several other kids toddled over toward Tess as she kneeled on the floor. "Ring around the rosie, pockets full of posies, ashes, ashes, we all fall down!"

All the giggling kids fell on top of Tess in the center of the floor.

" 'Gain, do 'gain," one tiny girl begged.

Reading her nametag, Tess said, "Okay, Waverly, we'll do it again. How about London Bridge?"

The kids all laughed, not really understanding the rules. But they willingly walked around in circles until the "bridge" came down.

Melissa walked over. "You really are good with kids. I know they could use help in here every couple of weeks. Maybe you and I could work together once a month."

"That'd be great." Tess found herself quietly excited. Maybe there was a place for her at this church after all, a place where she would fit right in. She lifted a chubby boy out of his crib and began to play pat-a-cake with him.

The nursery was so pleasant, with Noah's ark animals painted on the walls and bright red swings hanging from the ceiling. Grubby hands reached for the graham crackers that Melissa handed out, and Tess, who was on pacifier duty, made sure each baby had her own.

After snack time Melissa said, "We need to start sniffing in about ten minutes."

"What do you mean 'sniffing'?" she asked, confused.

"You know, sniffing the kids. To see if they need a diaper change. We don't change them all; only the ones who need it."

"Well, how do you tell?"

"You sniff. Behind the obvious spot. If they smell, they need to be changed, and we hand them to my mom so she can change their diapers."

"No way!" Tess said. She did her part, though, and it wasn't so bad until she found an offender. So much for powder and springtime.

Once all the kids were changed, they went back to playing. Then the parents came one by one to pick up their children. Melissa's mom called out the children's names as their parents arrived, and Tess and Melissa scooped up the kids to deliver them special express to the door. Afterward, the two girls picked up the toys.

"Where do you go to school?" Melissa asked, twisting her hair up into a ponytail holder as she sprayed Lysol on the big toys.

"At Coronado. How about you?" Tess answered.

"Yavapai."

"Why are you spraying those things?" Tess motioned to the Lysol can.

" 'Cause the kids drool all over them."

"Gross," Tess said.

"It's part of working here, picking up and spraying down afterward. I told Mom we wanted to work together once a month. She said, "Great." They'll put you on the list. And we'll get our own aprons with our names embroidered on them. Do you spell your name T-E-S-S?"

"Yeah." Tess smiled. She would have her own nursery apron. How fun. And Melissa was so nice.

"Will you call me and let me know what weeks we're working?" Tess asked.

"Sure," Melissa ripped a picture from one of the coloring books. It was Noah's ark. "How's this for notepaper?"

"More interesting than what I usually use," Tess said.

"What's your phone number?"

Tess told her, and Melissa wrote it down, saying, "Maybe we can get together sometime."

"Sure," Tess agreed, then looked up to see Erin at the

door. Sunday school must be over. Erin smiled at her. Tess froze. She hadn't even asked Erin if she could ride with Erin's family every week, and now she had committed herself to working in the nursery. She hoped it would be okay.

thirteen

Fajita Rapido's

Sunday Night, November 24

Later that day Tess called down the hall, "Mom, are you coming?" before slipping her feet into her black tennis shoes and lacing them up.

"Yes, I am. I'm not sure I'll eat much, but at least I can sit with you all." Her mom's voice sounded weary, but she was smiling as she peeked into Tess's room. Molly Thomas's lovely peach skin highlighted her shamrock-green eyes. Tess said a silent prayer that God would make her mom well soon and not let her have cancer. Tess prayed about that a lot these days.

"Dad's got the Jeep started; so let's go."

The family was driving to Fajita Rapido's, a new Mexican restaurant down the street.

As they headed out, Tyler said, "Look! They're starting to put up the Christmas decorations."

"At the mall, of course." The dimple in their dad's chin

deepened as he grinned. "Anything to start selling stuff sooner."

"I like Christmas," Tess said. "I can't wait. Can we put up lights on the house this year?"

"I suppose," her dad said. "Although we'll have to skip Christmas presents to pay the electricity bill with all those lights outside."

Tyler started to protest, but Tess saw that her dad was joking. She laughed, and they all joined in.

"Here we are!" After parking the car they pulled open the wooden double doors and were immediately greeted by the spicy air. The smell of sizzling shrimp fajitas tweaked Tess's nose. They were soon seated at a table for four. A bright red cloth gaily stretched over the square table, and a lazy Susan was set down in the middle.

"What's this?" Tyler said, spinning the lazy Susan around like a flat top.

"It's so we can put the condiments in the center to share, spinning them around to serve ourselves whatever we'd like next," Dad explained.

The waitress came by with four glasses of iced water, a floating lemon slice in each.

"Would you like some, Mom?" Tess asked.

"Yes, I think it might settle my stomach," her mother said.

Tess passed her one of the glasses and then passed out the others before serving herself. Tyler dumped three packages of sugar in his.

"Hey, that's rude, Tyler," said his dad. Then he asked everyone, "What do we want?"

"I don't think I'll eat anything, Jim. Just pick a little from whatever is ordered," Mrs. Thomas said. "So you guys get whatever you like."

When the waitress came, they ordered three entrees. "I'll have shrimp fajitas," Tess said, remembering the smell as she had walked into the restaurant. She loved the thought of the sweet, garlicky shrimp as they arrived hissing at the table.

"I'll have chicken, please," Tyler said.

Tess nodded. She loved chicken, too. Maybe she could trade him some shrimp for a piece of his moist chicken.

Dad ordered spicy beef. It tasted okay, as long as you picked out the nasty hot peppers. They could burn all the way down your throat if you ate one by mistake.

"Look at all the pretty lights!" Mrs. Thomas exclaimed.

A spray of colored lights showered the restaurant from above, lending a soft but festive glow to the room. The restaurant was crowded, and smelling everyone else's food tickled Tess's stomach. She was hungry. A mariachi band strummed in the corner, their long woven robes striped with bright turquoise blue, ocean green, and summer-sun yellow.

"Here you are! Be careful; the plates are hot." The waitress placed three blistering serving plates before them on the table. Each plate was a brown oval with a hot metal center. Piled on Tess's plate were tender, crispy pink shrimp grilled with butter. Ribbons of green and red bell peppers were laced in and around the shrimp, and tiny shards of softened onions speckled the peppers. Tyler's chicken looked tasty, too, but the peppers from Dad's plate sent a too-hot smell in Tess's direction.

The waitress soon returned with the condiments. She set each bowl or plate on the lazy Susan. First came the thick tomato salsa or *chile,* then smooth mounds of sour cream, a steaming basket of blue corn tortillas, and finally, one last bowl of a yellowish green spread.

"What's that?" Tyler asked. "Yuckamole?"

"It's *guac*amole," his mom answered.

"Well, I think it looks and tastes yucky, so I call it yuckamole," he answered. "But not the sour cream." He helped himself to a large scoop.

They spun the lazy Susan so everyone could share.

"Tess," someone called from across the room.

Tess turned around, scanning for anyone she knew. A waving hand drew her attention, and she saw Melissa. Tess smiled and waved back.

"Who's that?" Mr. Thomas asked pleasantly.

"Melissa. I met her at church this morning," Tess answered. "I worked in the toddler nursery with her and her mother."

"You didn't tell me you worked in the nursery, Tess," her mother scolded. "You need to tell me these things."

"Oh, yeah. Sorry. Well, I had a lot of fun, and they

asked me to work once a month. And," she said, scooping more shrimp on a fresh tortilla, " I get my own apron with my name embroidered on it."

"Hmm. I'll think about it. I'll need to talk with Melissa's mother first," Mrs. Thomas said.

Tess gulped. She hadn't thought about needing permission to work in the nursery.

"Did any babies puke on you?" Tyler asked

"Tyler, not at the dinner table," his mom said. Then she sat back. Tess thought her mom looked tired again.

"No, but I had to be a sniffer," Tess answered.

"What's a sniffer?" said her dad before spreading some more "yuckamole" on his fajita.

"You have to pick up each kid and sniff to see who needs a diaper change."

"Blimey, that's disgusting!" Tyler practically shouted, pinching his nose and making gagging noises. "You have to do that, and you want to go back? Next to you Big Al is downright civilized, old girl."

"Yeah, the kids were a lot of fun. And so was Melissa." She sneaked a look over at her new friend. Erin hadn't asked her about Melissa, and Tess hadn't said anything. She worried that Erin might feel bad if she had another church friend. Or what if Tess started to hang out with Melissa, too? Three friends hardly ever worked.

She remembered how her supposedly strong friendship with Colleen had dissolved as soon as Lauren entered the picture again. Colleen and Tess had been best friends last summer, or so Tess had thought. Then Lauren came back for school, and it became clear that Tess was the unwanted person in the group. Especially after Colleen and Lauren formed the nasty Coronado Club and hassled Tess. Oh, well. Erin wasn't like Lauren, and she wasn't Colleen. Everything would work out okay.

After dinner they ordered some sopapillas—hot, puffy pastries that were crisp on the outside and tender on the inside. Tess broke a little piece off one and dipped it into honey. "Want one, Mom?" she asked.

"No, I'm getting tired. We'd better get home so I can sleep. I have a big day tomorrow."

Oh, yeah. Tess had forgotten tomorrow was the test result day. What if it was cancer?

Later that night Tess sat under the firestorm of stars in her room, looking up at them in amazement. She remembered the "Star Light" poem and decided to whip out a piece of paper and rewrite it. After several attempts she settled on one.

"Star light, star bright, first star I see tonight, I believe that all will be all right because I trust God's love and might."

She slid out of bed and logged into her diary.

Dear God,

We had a really good time tonight, and I was glad Mom could come. Do you remember that verse my grandpa underlined in his Bible, before I was even born? Well, I underlined it in my Bible, too. You know, the new one Erin gave me. Psalm 56:3-4, "When I am afraid, I will trust you. I praise God for his word. I trust God. So I am not afraid." I feel sort of afraid, but I know you can take care of it. Please take care of Mom, Jesus. I'm afraid she's going to die like Solomon did.

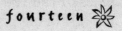

fourteen

Something Up Your Sleeve?

Monday, November 25

"How are you feeling today?" Tess asked Erin. They hadn't had a chance to talk much this morning, personally anyway. Now lunchtime allowed them a little peace and quiet.

"Okay. What do you mean?" Erin asked, biting into her cheese pizza.

"I mean about Solomon. You know."

"Oh, that. Well, I feel pretty sad still, but at least my grandparents aren't going to sell the ranch. How's your mom?"

"I don't know." Tess shifted her weight, folding one leg under her. She slurped down some chocolate milk before answering. "Her test results come back today. So I'll know after school."

"Do you still want to come over for dinner and to study tonight?"

"I guess so. Unless it's really bad. I'll come about 5:30

unless I call you. I hope I don't have to." Tess pushed the rest of her pizza away, not even touching the chocolate chip cookies. "I'm not hungry."

"Can I have your cookies?" Erin asked.

Tess sighed. "Yes. I don't know how you stay so skinny."

"Good genes, I guess." Erin smiled, biting off half a cookie as she glanced at the table behind her. "Hey, there's Scott."

"Yes, I know. Look at those guys! How can you like him?" Since Tess faced Scott's table, she had been watching all along. Erin turned around just in time to see Scott guzzle his milk and then force it out his nose all over his lunch tray.

Erin smiled and said, "Yeah, it's pretty disgusting. But Scott is cute. My brother is disgusting, too, and you think he's pretty great. And he's not even cute."

"I bet he doesn't let milk come out his nostrils," Tess challenged her. Tess couldn't image Tom being so immature.

"No, but he uses his bare hand as a flyswatter," Erin said, polishing off the cookie. "And he smashes them dead."

"Gross," Tess said. Still, it didn't seem as bad as Scott's behavior. And Tom *was* cute. Too bad Erin didn't realize it. Tess guessed she understood. It would be hard for her to see how anyone could have a crush on Tyler, no matter how much she liked him as a brother.

"Speaking of Scott, are you excited about the Thanksgiving program this week?" Erin asked.

"I guess so," Tess answered. "I feel better now that we have all the stuff worked out with Scott and Bill. I hope my parents can come."

"Me, too," Erin agreed.

Just then Katie and Joann came up to their table.

"Hi, you two!" Katie said as she and Joann plopped down into chairs. "Since you guys let us copy you, you know, to be Secret Sisters," she held up her new charm bracelet and clinked it against Joann's bracelet, "we thought we'd ask if you wanted to do a craft fair with us next month."

"What is it?" Erin asked, picking at her apple stem.

"Well, my mom is in charge of the Christmas craft fair held at the Saguaro Community Center, and she said we could have a booth. Lots of craft people sell all kinds of stuff, and there's food and music and everything. Each year they hold a raffle and give away a trip, too. We get to enter twice for free if we have a booth."

Tess couldn't remember when she had seen Katie in such a take-charge mode and Joann so laid back. "What's a booth? What do you do?" Tess asked.

"Well," Katie continued, "we make some crafts, and then we decorate our booth and sell the stuff we made. Last year I earned all my Christmas money at the fair. I crocheted bookmarks and put little wiggly eyes on them. They didn't take me very long to make, and I sold them for a dollar each. After I paid Mom back for the yarn and eyes, I had almost seventy dollars left."

"Seventy dollars! Wow! What do you think?" Tess turned to Erin.

"Well, what are you making this year?" Erin asked.

"Katie and I are buying plain pottery flower pots and painting them," Joann explained. "We'll paint flowers and rainbows, and I do whales pretty good. Then, when someone orders one, we'll paint her name on it so she has a personalized container to grow flowers in this spring. Plus, we might do personalized stationery. I got some paper and some stamps at the craft store. I want to get some gold embossing powder, but it's eight dollars, so I need to see if Mom will loan it to me."

"Yeah, that sounds fun. If we can think of a craft," Erin said. "Mom has some craft books at home. Tess, maybe when you come over tonight we can look through them and decide what to do."

"Good plan. Let's do it," Tess said. It would take hours of baby-sitting the Kim boys to earn seventy dollars. She had started to baby-sit last month, and the two boys were her first job. They were okay but a lot of work. Crafts seemed easier.

"All right. Go home tonight and ask your parents, and if they say okay, let me know tomorrow. I'll tell my mom, and she'll save us a booth. Want to go outside?" Katie stood up.

"Okay," Erin said, scooping her trash onto her tray. "What do you say, Tess?"

"Okay." Tess folded a napkin over her dead piece of pizza. "I'll get my sweatshirt out of my locker, then I'll meet you." Good thing she had brought her sweatshirt folded up in the bottom of her backpack. November had suddenly turned cold.

✳

After lunch they went back to the classroom and started to work on math. It was long division, and Tess finished early. She cracked open her desk to pull out a book. After she had read a few pages, she heard Erin whistle softly at her. Tess looked over.

Erin was pointing at Tess's arm.

Tess didn't get it. "What?" she whispered.

"Your arm," Erin whispered back, trying not to get caught talking.

"What's wrong with it?"

"There's a big bulge in your sleeve," she whispered.

Tess reached up her sleeve and felt around carefully. Something was up her sleeve. Grabbing hold of the edge of whatever was in there, she whipped it out in front of her.

Underpants! Pink underpants with a white lacy ruffle almost flew out of her hand! Quickly Tess stuffed them into her desk, glancing around to see if anyone had been watching, but most people were still scratching out answers to their math problems. The underpants must have stuck to the inside of her sweatshirt, and when she put it on after lunch her underwear was lurking there to embarrass her.

Tess whispered back to Erin, "I guess that's why I'm supposed to use the cling sheets in the drier. I skipped that part when I was helping do the laundry. Don't tell anyone, okay?" Her face was still beefy red. How was she going to sneak underpants out of her desk and into her backpack?

"Don't worry," Erin whispered back. "I'll write you a note." After scribbling a bit, Erin passed the paper to Tess. It read, "At my ninth birthday I had friends and relatives over at the same time for my party. My Aunt Jessie bought me Tweetie Bird underpants, and I had to open the present in front of everyone. It was so embarrassing! I know how you feel."

Tess giggled. For some reason, you always felt better if someone else was embarrassed, too.

Ms. Martinez asked the class to move on to the next topic, which would be the last for the school day. Then Tess was off for home—and to hear about her mother's test results.

fifteen

Test Results

Monday Afternoon, November 25

Tyler kicked a rock from the sidewalk into the street as they walked home in the light wind. Tess pulled her sweatshirt tight around her and flipped the hood over her head.

"So, what do you think?" she asked him.

"About what?" he answered, snapping his gum.

"I bet Sherlock Holmes keeps his gum in his mouth," she answered. "I mean about Mom."

"I don't know. I guess we'll find out soon enough. Just don't start bawling or anything."

"I'm not going to do that. Give me a break," Tess answered.

They rounded the corner and approached their house.

"Dad's home. Maybe it's bad, or he would have gone back to work," Tess said.

"I don't know. Hey, next time you wash clothes could

you put in a drier sheet? My pants were clinging to my socks all day." Tyler leaned over and pulled down his pants cuffs. "I say, it can be a bit annoying."

"Yeah, I know." Tess opened the back door and called, "Hello, anyone home?"

"We're in the living room," her dad answered. "Come on in here, both of you."

Tess kicked off her shoes and looked at her brother. His eyes were wide, but he didn't say anything. They hardly ever sat in the living room.

As they went into the room, their mom and dad were sitting together on the couch, almost smooshed together in the middle. Mrs. Thomas had circles under her eyes, but she smiled as they came in. They sat on the floor in front of the couch. The beige carpet felt soft and clean against Tess's hand as she nervously rubbed the fibers.

"Your mother and I have something to tell you," her dad began. Tyler and Tess waited quietly. "You know that the doctor was to have the test results back today. Well, they all came back negative for almost everything we were looking at."

"You mean Mom doesn't have cancer?" Tess jumped up in joy.

"No, no, I don't have cancer. Why ever did you think that?" Mrs. Thomas asked.

"We just thought that since Grandpa Pat had that, you might, too," Tyler replied.

"Well, what's wrong then?" Tess settled down, hoping it was nothing worse.

"Well, when the call came back negative," their dad answered, "the doctor had a hunch he might know what was going on. So he asked Mom to come in today for a last quick test in his office. I went with her, and this time, the test came back positive."

"Positive for what?" Tyler asked fearfully.

"We're going to have a baby!" Their mother smiled, tired but happy.

"You're kidding!" Tyler said. "A baby?"

"Yes. We're just as surprised as you guys. We didn't even suspect that was a possibility, since Dad and I thought we couldn't have any more children after you, Tyler. And I was never so sick with you two. Even though I am sick, the baby and I are fine, and in a month or so I'll be back to my same old self. With a baby inside, of course. What do you think, Tess?"

"I'm really glad you aren't sick, Mom. I-I'm just surprised about the baby. I mean, I never guessed." It was true. She felt glad that her mom was well and sort of excited about a baby but sort of embarrassed, too. Wasn't her mother too old for this?

"The idea will take a while for us all to get used to, I'm sure," Mr. Thomas said. "But we'll make adjustments before the baby is born at the end of June."

"Can you come to the Thanksgiving program Wednesday?" Tess asked.

"I think so," her mother answered. "But probably not Dad. He's missed a lot of work the past few weeks."

"Well, I have only one thing to say." Tyler stood up,

putting his hands on his hips. "And I am absolutely serious."

"What is it, honey?" Mrs. Thomas looked a little worried.

"I am no way, no how, never going to sniff this baby. I don't care if it is my own brother or sister. Tess enjoys it and will have plenty of experience."

They all broke out laughing, and Tess threw a pillow at her brother. "I'd be glad to pass on my sniffing techniques."

He threw a pillow back. "You can keep your techniques. The only thing I care about sniffing for is a bloodhound to help me solve mysteries."

Their dad interrupted. "Is it too cold out, or should we grab a cone at the ice cream shop before dropping Tess off at Erin's?"

"Steady on, old boy. It's never too cold for ice cream!" Tyler answered, and Tess agreed.

She went to change clothes and brush her hair before meeting them all at the car.

Later, at the ice cream shop, Tess asked Tyler, "Don't you want to try something besides vanilla? It's so boring!"

"Why switch horses when you know one that will win the race?" Tyler asked, chomping down on his cone.

Mrs. Thomas smiled. "I sort of like vanilla myself," she answered. "I think I feel good enough to have a cone, too."

They sat in the bright pink restaurant, eating their

cones for a couple of minutes. As they swiveled on the stools at the counter, Tess told them about the embarrassing underwear incident at school.

"Hoo-hoo, I thought my pants cuffs were bad!" Ty laughed. "Wait till I tell Big Al!"

"Mom!" Tess wailed.

"You'll do no such thing, young man," his mother warned. "I'll be feeling well enough to do the laundry again soon, honey. I do appreciate all your work." She smiled and ruffled Tess's hair.

Tess smiled back, glad her mom was all right. *Thank you, Lord,* she prayed silently. *You are right. I can trust you. You always do what is best.*

"Say, we'd better get going if Tess is to make it to Erin's in time for dinner," Dad said.

They finished up their ice cream and pitched the napkins into the trash. Tess pushed the water fountain button for Tyler, squirting him with a little extra blast as he leaned over.

"Gotcha!" she giggled good-naturedly.

He smiled. "Don't forget. I owe you one." He held open the door, and they walked out of the store.

"Hey, lady, want a kitten?" A boy about Tyler's age and his mother were standing next to the phone booth outside the ice cream parlor. He held a wicker picnic basket with three fluffy kittens peeking out from under its lid.

"Oh look!" Tess ran over to pet them. A tiny orange tabby seemed to smile at her. "May I hold him?" she asked the boy.

"It's a her, but sure, you can pick her up," he answered.

Tess scooped her up. She was barely big enough to fill Tess's hand. Soft fur tickled between her fingers, and the kitten's rough tongue licked Tess's knuckles as the kitty squirmed in her hand.

"Oh, Mom, can we get one? Please?" Tess pleaded.

"What about Hercules?" Tyler asked. "A cat might eat him."

"I'd watch her. Oh please, Mom?"

"Honey, we're going to have enough baby stuff to keep us busy without adding a pet. I think the answer has to be no for now."

"But look at her. She's so cute. She's so adorable. What if they don't find a family for her?"

"A cute kitty like that? They'll find her a home. Come on, set her down, and let's go."

Tess rubbed the kitten's satiny smooth ears. Then she had an idea. "Mom, I think I know what we can do!"

She whispered her idea to her mother, who nodded her head in agreement. Now, if only Tess could get the right person to say yes.

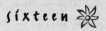

sixteen

Star Light

Monday Evening, November 25

"Hey, you, stay still!" Tess struggled to keep the wriggling blanket in her arms as she lifted one hand to ring the doorbell. As soon as Mrs. Janssen opened the door, Tess waved good-bye to her parents, and they sped off.

"Do you have her?" Erin's mom grinned.

"Yes, I do. She's in the blanket. Where's Erin?" Tess asked.

"In her room. This is good timing. She was just crying over Solomon. I'll let you surprise her, then bring the surprise out to meet me, too."

Tess smiled broadly and headed down the hall to Erin's room. Music blared through the closed door. After Tess knocked loudly a few times, Erin turned down the volume and answered.

"Hi! I'm glad you could come." She smiled, but her eyes were still red. "What's in there?" Erin pointed to the large Navajo blanket in Tess's arms. Erin's eyes grew large as the blanket squirmed.

Tess handed over the bundle, and as she did, her surprise leaped out from her confines.

"A kitty!" Erin squealed. "When did you get it?" She scooped up the baby cat, whose tabby fur was the color of orange marmalade.

"She's yours. Surprise!" Tess laughed.

Erin's jaw dropped, and she gaped at Tess. "What do you mean, she's mine?"

"Well, we saw this boy holding a cute little basket of kittens outside the ice cream store. I went over and held this one. She was the sweetest thing, and I didn't want to let her go. My parents said I couldn't keep her—I'll tell you why in a minute—but she was so warm and trusting. Then I had a great idea! You needed someone to cheer you up after losing Solomon. And you said you never had a pet of your own. I know she's not a horse," Tess finished a bit shyly, "but I hope she'll do."

"Oh, Tess, nothing could ever replace Solomon. I wouldn't even try. But I love kittens, and this one could be my very own. That is," Erin stopped, frowning a bit, "if my mom and dad will let me keep her."

"Silly," Tess said, "I wouldn't have brought her without asking your mom and dad. I called them from the shopping center before coming over. They've already said yes!"

"All right!" Erin practically cheered. She nuzzled the kitten close to her cheek. "Come on, baby. Let's introduce you to the rest of the family." The kitty mewed in response, and Erin led the way out to the family room.

"Thanks, Mom!" She ran to her mother and hugged her. "This is the best thing that has happened to me all month."

"Let's see that little bundle." Mrs. Janssen held out her hand, and Erin set the kitten into her mother's palm.

"You sweet thing," Erin's mom whispered to the kitten. "Let's keep you away from Butch for a while, till you're able to fend for yourself. Well, Erin, what are you going to name her?"

"I don't know. I have to think about it."

"How's your mother, Tess?" Mrs. Janssen asked, switching off the stereo so she could focus on the girls.

"She's doing much better, thanks," Tess answered. "Actually, she's going to have a baby." She looked toward the floor and kicked her toe into the rug.

"My goodness, what news! When did she find out?" Mrs. Janssen asked. Erin, for the second time in ten minutes, stood there with her mouth wide open in surprise.

"They just told her today. They thought she had some bad kind of anemia or something that makes your blood weak. But she didn't. She's pregnant. And the baby will come at the end of June."

"Congratulations. Now, I'd better get supper on if we're ever going to eat. Dad will be home tonight." She smiled at Erin. "He and Josh went to pick up Tom at basketball practice."

"Yippee!" Erin said. As a chef, Ned Janssen worked a

lot of nights but was trying to spend more time at home. "We'll be in the back," Erin said, cradling the kitty and leading Tess toward the backyard.

A wide, woven hammock stretched between two gnarled pecan trees, and the girls both climbed in. Swinging gently in the dimming afternoon light, they giggled as the kitten crawled all over them, trying to escape into the backyard.

"I don't think you want to escape, you little fur ball." Erin guarded the kitten, keeping her from falling off. "Guess what?" She poked at her friend.

"What?" Tess answered.

"I asked my mom if I could do the craft booth, and she said yes. So I called up Katie and told her to save us a booth. You'll never guess who else is having a booth."

"Who?" Tess asked, sitting up in curiosity.

"The Coronado Club!"

"You're joking," Tess said. The Coronado Club? The group of popular sixth-grade girls? Tess had been good friends with Colleen, their president, over the summer. At the beginning of the school year the club members had wanted Tess to do some nasty tricks to get into the group, but when she refused, they played mean tricks on her instead.

"No, I'm not joking. I can't imagine their doing crafts, but trust them to be right in the middle of anything fun. Who cares? We'll have fun anyway. As long as they don't try to mess it up."

"Which they will," Tess said nervously. "I haven't asked my mom, but I'm sure she'll let me join the booth with you guys. What should we make?" She picked at the hammock cord, unraveling it a bit. She hoped Colleen and Lauren wouldn't interfere too much with their fun.

"I don't know. Let's look at Mom's craft book after dinner. But first we have a more important job," Erin said, fingering the kitten's soft baby fur between her thumb and first two fingers.

"What's that?" Tess rubbed the cat's head.

"To figure out a name for this little one, of course. How about 'Fireball,' since her fur looks like firelight?"

"Naw, too grown up," Tess said. "But speaking of light, that reminds me of a poem I wrote the other night. Want to read it?" She fished the paper out of her pocket. She had brought it along, eager to show Erin that her faith was growing.

Erin read, "'Star light, star bright, first star I see tonight, I know that all will be all right because I trust God's love and might.' That's really cool, Tess."

"Thanks. I didn't even know Mom would be okay when I wrote it, and she is! And even though Solomon had to be put to sleep, he did live to be old, and your grandparents aren't going to sell the ranch."

"True," Erin said, snuggling into the kitten's soft neck fur. "And I got this little one, the best gift ever, from my best friend ever, my Secret Sister." She smiled at Tess. "Hey! I know, we can name her Starlight!"

"Now that's a good name," Tess agreed. They both sat up as they heard the Suburban pull into the driveway.

"That must be my dad and the boys," Erin said. "Let's introduce them to Starlight."

"Okay," Tess agreed, smoothing back her hair.

The early evening stars winked their approval of the kitten's new name. Desert dust rose to greet the setting sun, painting the soft blue sky with watercolor purple and rose.

Tess twisted her bracelet and whispered, "Thank you, Lord," toward the pinking sky. "For my mom, and the baby, and Erin, and everything." Slipping her feet back into her shoes, she followed her pal into the house.

Have More Fun!!

Visit the official website at:
www.secretsisters.com

There are lots of activities, exciting contests, and a chance for YOU to tell me what you'd like to see in future Secret Sisters books! AND—be the first to know when the next Secret Sisters book will be at your bookstore by signing up for the instant e-mail update list. See you there today!

If you don't have access to the Internet, please write to me at:

Sandra Byrd
P.O. Box 2115
Gresham, OR 97030

Would you like to own your own Secret Sisters charms? You can buy a set that includes each of the eight silver charms Tess and Erin own—a heart, ponies, star, angel, Bible, paintbrush, dolphin, and flower bouquet. Please send $8 (includes shipping and handling) to: Parables Charms, P.O. Box 2115, Gresham, OR 97030. Quantities are limited.

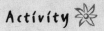

Snack Attack

Next time you and your Secret Sister take a field trip, even if it's just to the park, pack each other a snack attack bag.

Decorate a plain paper bag with watercolors or markers or colored chalk from the art or office supply store. Then fill with snacks she's sure to enjoy.

You might choose one of these themes, or develop one of your own!

Garden Patch

- Baby carrots
- Tiny tub of dip
- Can of V-8
- Whole-wheat minibagel
- Vegetable cream cheese
- Gummy worms

Tea Party

- Crustless sandwich
- Bottle of iced tea
- Sugar cubes
- Lemon drops
- Brownies

Candy Store

- Candy necklace
- Circus peanuts
- M and M's
- Carton of milk

Solve this puzzle to learn more about what you'll read inside Book Four!

Across

2 Tiny abode with small furniture
5 Gift
6 Place to write private thoughts
7 Popular girls' club
8 Tess and Erin make to sell at fair
10 Strong disagreement
11 Cash
12 Divine messenger

Down

1 Holiday celebrating Jesus' birth
2 Place for city cowgirls
3 Not brothers
4 Error
5 Opposite of wealthy
9 Tyler's gross friend

**Look for the other titles in
Sandra Byrd's Secret Sisters Series!
Available at your local Christian bookstore**

Available Now:

#1 *Heart to Heart:* When the exclusive Coronado Club invites Tess Thomas to join, she thinks she'll do anything to belong—until she finds out just how much is required.

#2 *Twenty-One Ponies:* There are plenty of surprises—and problems—in store for Tess. But a native-American tale teaches her just how much God loves her.

#3 *Star Light:* Tess's mother becomes seriously ill, and Tess's new faith is tested. Can she trust God with the big things as well as the small?

#4 *Accidental Angel:* Tess and Erin have great plans for their craft-fair earnings. But after their first big fight will they still want to spend it together? And how does Tess become the "accidental" angel?

#5 *Double Dare:* A game of "truth or dare" leaves Tess feeling like she doesn't measure up. Will making the gymnastics team prove she can excel?

#6 *War Paint:* Tess must choose between running for Miss Coronado and entering the school mural-painting contest with Erin. There are big opportunities—and a big blowout with the Coronado Club.

#7 *Holiday Hero:* This could be the best Spring Break ever—or the worst. Tess's brother, Tyler, is saved from disaster, but can the sisters rescue themselves from even bigger problems?

#8 *Petal Power:* Ms. Martinez is the most beautiful bride in the world, and the sisters are there to help her get married. When trouble strikes her honeymoon plans, Tess and Erin must find a way to help save them.

#9 *First Place:* The Coronado Club insists Tess won't be able to hike across the Grand Canyon and plans to tell the whole sixth grade about it at Outdoor School. Tess looks confident but worries in silence, not wanting to share the secret that could lead to disaster.

#10 *Camp Cowgirl:* The Secret Sisters are ready for an awesome summer camp at a Tucson horse ranch, until something—and someone—interferes. What happens if your best friend wants other friends, and you're not sure, but you might too?

The Secret Sister Handbook: 101 Cool Ideas for You and Your Best Friend! It's fun to read about Tess and Erin and just as fun to do things with your own Secret Sister! This book is jam-packed with great things for you to do together all year long.

Available September 2000:

#11 *Picture Perfect:* Tess and Erin sign up for modeling school, but will they be able to go? Could they ever get any modeling assignments? Along the way the Secret Sisters find out that things aren't always just as they seem, a fact confirmed when Tess's mother has her baby.

#12 *Indian Summer:* When Tess and Erin sign up to go on their first mission trip—to the Navajo reservation—they plan to teach Vacation Bible School. What do a young Navajo girl and Tess have in common? In the end Tess has to make some of the most important choices in her new Christian life.